The Master Mechanic

A Sheridan County Mystery

Erin Lark Maples

Dedication

To my Uncle Jeff,
a fan of classic cars and storytelling.

1

Elizabeth flapped a kitchen towel in front of the fire alarm and prayed for cooperative silence as she inhaled the scent of toasted rosemary, caramelized brown sugar, and butter. When the timer buzzed, she removed the baker's sheet of roasted nuts from the oven. The brown morsels were shiny with a thin glaze, like jewels. She set the tray on the range to cool.

"Smells like a perfect death," Enid called from across the hall. The owner of Beans & Biscuits was sequestered in her tiny office, reviewing orders.

"I'll take that as a compliment, I guess?" With a shake of the tray, Elizabeth rattled the nuts. She levered a spatula underneath the mix and tipped a portion into a small ramekin. She took the dish into Enid's office and set it atop one of the many leaning towers of books. "Here. Give them a moment to cool."

Enid took the proffered dish and held it under her nose. She took a deep breath and closed her eyes. "Decadent. Reminds me of backpacking after high school. My best friend and I took off across Europe. Two hundred dollars between us and no specific plans."

Elizabeth lifted an eyebrow. "Go on."

Enid crunched down on a handful of the snack mix. "Mel was deathly allergic to nuts."

"How does someone know if they are deathly allergic to anything if they haven't died from it yet?"

"Most would rather believe a doctor than risk it, I think."

"Fair." Elizabeth returned to the small kitchen. The space held a set of stainless steel appliances, tubs of baking ingredients, and dishes. She continued her preparations. Above the rack of pots and pans was a Kiss the Cook sign. A commercial mixer held court in one corner. Elizabeth took in the sight, willing that one day, she would have her own.

Elizabeth turned on a burner and set a small pan atop the blue flame. When the pan was warm, she added a few cardamom pods. Every few seconds, she gave the pan a shake. The pods darkened, and she removed them from the heat. With the side of a knife, she crushed the pods against a cutting board.

Enid had granted Elizabeth after hours kitchen access. Along with her brother, Elizabeth had a big task. They needed to prepare the menu for Blau Brewing's first big catering event. Casey had booked the gig, but to be legitimate, they needed a real kitchen. Rentals were more than she or her brother could afford for their fledgling business. Enid was a saving grace.

Beans was Enid's breakfast and lunch cafe on Sheridan's busy Main Street. They did brisk business into the afternoon. Other than the Thursday night knitting circle and the occasional book club, Enid closed up shop each day at three. She'd offered the kitchen space to the Blau siblings any evening they liked. Enid joked it was selfish on her part. The owner would not take any money in exchange for using the space. Instead, she asked for her own plate of hors d'oeuvres.

"I see your point," Enid said from the doorway. She tucked the empty dish into the dishwasher rack among the plates, cups, and bowls. Enid gave Elizabeth's plastic container of raw nuts a brief shake.

"For my aunt it was bees. Test you somehow, I suppose. That summer it ate Mel up to miss so much of the European cuisine. They put nuts in everything. At pastry shops, she could only get as close as the plaza outside a patisserie. Any closer and her eyes would puff up and her throat would constrict. She looked ready to cry one day while she watched me scarf forkfuls of Marjolaine. I licked each of my fingers in delight. Right in front of her. Poor thing."

"Cruel," Elizabeth teased. "Best friends aren't for torturing. Especially not over pastry." Elizabeth opened a container of dates at her elbow and plucked one out. She fished out the pit before replacing it with a roasted almond from the pan. The hazelnuts would go into the cookies. Walnuts, cashews, and peanuts would be a snack mix for the tables.

Enid consulted a laminated order sheet hung on the door. With a grease pencil she found tied to a string taped near the list and ticked a couple of boxes. "The afternoon we walked the Seine, she told me that if she was ever kidnapped and held hostage, she'd request death by anaphylaxis."

Elizabeth flicked her gaze to her wrist, but the latex glove covered her watch face. Wherever Casey was, he was late. "In Paris? How...romantic?"

"Her last meal." Enid shrugged and swiped a plump cashew from the pan. She held the nut up to her face and peered at it, a close inspection. "If she had to die, let it be by something she'd lusted after her whole life. Very Parisian."

A brisk knock on the door echoed through the empty cafe. "I'll get it," Enid said, and left the kitchen to return a moment later with Jo, Elizabeth's best friend and alleged babysitter for the evening.

"I got halfway home before your son alerted me to the fact that I'd neglected to bring his giraffe." Jo spoiled Rhett, Elizabeth's only child, with a new animal figurine every chance she could. Last week's gift was the two-year old's new favorite. "He kept reaching for the back windshield and straining against his straps. I installed him with Clint and zipped back over here to fetch it."

"Let me peek behind the benches," Enid said. "Kids are always dropping stuff back there."

Jo and her husband, Clint, were the nearest version of grandparents Rhett had in his life. The pair reveled in their roles. Elizabeth was grateful for the babysitting, a necessity to maintain a job. Even more, she counted her blessings daily for the incredible love and care the Wolfs poured into her son's life.

"He loves that thing," Elizabeth said. She consulted an ingredients list in front of her. "I don't know if it's the neck or the spots, but it's replaced the antelope for the top spot in the barn."

"Found it!" Enid returned, triumphant, from the cafe. Several curls escaped her emerald headband, which tipped askew atop her head. "Had to crawl under some tables. Guessing it tumbled off when y'all were here earlier. Let me give it a quick wash." She took the long-necked animal to the sink for a bath.

"How goes the prep?" Jo picked up the various containers on the steel countertop to read their labels. Her mass of thick hair roped upward in a twist, threads of gray streaking through. She nodded in approval at Elizabeth's sheets of directions spread across the industrial steel."

"Checking that I brought everything?" Elizabeth teased her friend. The week before, the two women had spent an afternoon and a carafe of iced tea making a list of every ingredient and tool needed for the event. Jo was a world-class list maker, the kind of person who believed in preparation.

Jo unscrewed the cap from a slim bottle and sniffed at its contents. "More like it never occurred to me to own something like sesame oil. Or what was that fancy stuff for the soaked cherries?"

"Maraschino liqueur?"

"Too many syllables for our house. For me, really. Clint actually eats that stuff up."

Elizabeth spooned dabs of goat cheese into the seam of each date. "I'm getting there. I'd be a lot further along if my wayward brother would get his tush over here though."

Enid held out the washed and dried toy to Jo. "I'll get out of your hair, so you can get to it. You've got the spare key. Break a leg. Then, come by tomorrow to let me know how it went."

"Thanks," Elizabeth said. She waved a gloved hand, sticky with dates, at the woman's retreating form.

Jo picked up one of the ingredient lists and paired it with the recipe. "You've got the dates going. Nuts look done. Mushrooms?"

"Already stuffed. Pesto pastry rolls, too." Elizabeth gestured to the plastic-wrapped trays along the counter. "Fruit tarts cooled and went into the fridge. Casey smoked the trout for the crackers yesterday, so we'll plate those on site. My next item to tackle is the venison. Thanks for that, by the way."

"We often end up with more than we can eat—or that I am willing to cook. Come summer, I'm happy to pawn some off on an honest taker."

Elizabeth pulled the defrosted meat from the refrigerator. "I am going to pair it with fig paste and wrap it in the grape leaves."

"You definitely took the theme to heart in your planning. I confess, I never thought about what ancient Romans ate until this party."

"Casey said it was a themed murder mystery. Would be kind of strange for gods and goddesses to be downing hotdogs. Ruin the energy."

"Pretty sure they would have appreciated a Chicago Dog like the rest of us," Jo said. A frantic rapping at the door startled the women. "I'll check it. Watch, Enid locked herself out. You stay put."

Elizabeth heard the jangle of the front door. A figure rushed past the kitchen door and into the tiny restroom. Retching noises came through the doorway, followed by a flush of the toilet and a groan.

"I found Casey," Jo called.

2

"Go home," Jo said. "Or to Danny's. Let him take care of you. You're in no shape to stay here." Danny was Casey's current love interest.

Casey groaned and rested a shoulder on the kitchen door jamb. His face was pale, forehead beaded with sweat. After he'd been sick in the restroom, the sink had run for a bit, followed by the rattle of the paper towel holder. A few minutes later, he stumbled over to the kitchen.

"Don't come any closer," he said. Her brother, typically the picture of mountain-man health, held up a hand, panting. "I don't know if it's catching." Jo handed Casey a glass of water. "Thank you." He sipped from it and closed his eyes. "I brought the trout. The cooler is in the cafe."

Elizabeth knitted her brows together. "You look like something Leia dragged in from the yard, half-dead and covered in slobber." She willed the panic building in her chest to settle. There wasn't time for this. Casey getting sick was not on any of Jo's checklists.

"I feel worse."

"What happened to you?"

Casey rested his head on the door frame. "I don't know if it was the egg salad or the sprouts, but yesterday's lunch did not sit right." He clutched at his gut and winced.

"Jo's right." Elizabeth pursed her lips and put her hands on her hips. "You can't stay. Whatever it is, we can't have you near other people's food."

Casey shook his head, a slow and pitiful protest. "I can't leave now. What about the party? There's so much to do."

Elizabeth pressed her hands to her cheeks, leaving sticky spots. She couldn't manage an entire event herself. Yet, all the food, the hours, and the client would be gone if they canceled. "I guess I'll just...do it all myself. Somehow. But Casey, if this stomach bug doesn't finish you off, I might. I can't believe you got us into this mess."

Jo dropped the giraffe into a paper sack and folded the top over several times. She pressed the bag to Casey's chest. "Drop this off on our front porch on your way home. Do not knock. I'll tell Clint to look for it in a half hour. And to wash it. In case it wasn't the egg salad, I don't want you getting either of those boys sick. Then, go home. Call Danny and feel better." Clint was Jo's husband, on babysitting duty for the evening.

Elizabeth crossed her arms over her chest and gave her shoulders a squeeze. She regarded the trays of finished food and the stack of recipes she'd yet to begin. This wasn't an intimate gathering of a half dozen people, a dinner at her house. This was a company party, with a theme and all. To show up with half the food prepared would be the end of their new business venture before it could start. But she couldn't manage this on her own.

Jo pushed Casey toward the front door. The bell chimed again as he exited. Jo returned to the kitchen and reached for one of the clean aprons on a hook near the door. She wrapped the straps around her waist and tied them behind her back. "Don't stand there staring at me like a stunned goldfish. Put me to work."

Elizabeth blinked, then slid a cutting board to Jo, then passed her a bowl of vegetables. "Veggie platter?"

"Can do." Jo stepped to the double sink. She slipped her wedding rings off and added them to her necklace. They dangled next to the horseshoe pendent. Jo turned on the tap and lathered up.

"You are a saint," Elizabeth said. "With Casey out my nerves have officially blitzed out."

"What are friends for? Besides, catering seems a lot like cooking for family. A very large one." The thop-thop-thop of the knife against the cutting board made a staccato rhythm. Jo arranged carrot spears and bell pepper strips atop a shallow, bamboo dish. Each bent around the next, curved rays filling the circular platter.

Midday heat shimmered off the sidewalks outside the window. An air conditioner kicked on with a low hum. The women worked in otherwise companionable silence.

When Jo finished, she stepped back to admire her work. A spiral of veggies fanned out from the center where a dip bowl would rest. "Tell you what. That was satisfying. No wonder y'all want to break into this business."

"For the record, this is all Casey's fault," Elizabeth said. "'Get a catering gig,' he said. 'It will be easy,' he said. Hah!" She stabbed a stuffed date with a toothpick and placed it among the others.

"Come on, now. As far as typical office parties go, this one sounds fun! A murder mystery? The most Clint's office ever did was a round of bowling in town. Whose party is it? Can I be the murderer?"

"You're a bit eager on the murder uptake, my friend." Elizabeth arranged the now-stuffed dates in a ceramic dish. "I don't know who it's for. Casey made the booking. I've got the address. Oh, and the costumes."

"Costumes?" Jo had moved from vegetables to slicing bread for crostini. Using Enid's loaf slicer, she drew the baguette across the blade. Neat, thin rounds of bread piled below the machine. "I better be something good. Can't see myself passing trays of hors d'oeuvres in a *T. rex* suit."

"A murder mystery with dinosaurs? Wouldn't that be nothing but the herbivores accusing the omnivores?"

"Gives new meaning to the phrase 'dog-eat-dog.'"

Elizabeth snapped off her gloves and held her face in her hands. "What if I can't handle this? We've got to leave in an hour, and I haven't finished the appetizers. The party starts at seven. We have to set up early, and it's halfway to Buffalo."

"Easy there, my friend. No need to put the cart before the horse. We've got a solid sixty minutes before we have to leave. If anyone can do this, it's us. You've got the Josephine Candelaria Patented Organizational System at your personal disposal. Don't quit while you're ahead."

"Did I mention the costumes?"

Jo pitched one eyebrow upward. "So, that wasn't a joke?"

"Casey's idea. I'm Vesta, and he was going to be Bacchus. There are outfits in a box in the hallway. And masks."

Jo sucked in her cheeks, then nodded. "In for a penny, in for a pound, as my father used to say."

Elizabeth looked to her friend. "Thank you. I owe you one. Or six."

"Don't thank me yet. I'm starting a tab."

3

Roads skirted fence lines, then disappeared into the shadows of the afternoon. Elizabeth identified two hawks and an owl atop phone poles. The birds surveyed the area, gargoyle-like, on the otherwise deserted roads. They crossed a tiny bridge over Rock Creek and headed up a short hill, Jo's vehicle kicking up dust. At the crest, they'd come to the address on Casey's note with dusk on their heels. At Elizabeth's prompt, Jo angled her SUV off the dusty road. She sucked in her breath at the sight of a driveway fronted with a lodgepole arch.

"Been here before?" Elizabeth appraised her friend's knuckles, white against the black steering wheel.

"Sort of," Jo said, then swallowed. "It's been a while."

Jo had insisted on driving. Elizabeth's car couldn't hold half of what they needed to haul, and Casey's truck was back at Cloud Nine Ranch. Elizabeth riding shotgun meant she could rehash her setup strategy with little distraction. The fear-tinged hesitation in Jo's voice shook Elizabeth from her mental rehearsal.

Casey had scribbled down an address that lay north of Buffalo. The spread was an expanse of ranch land west of I-90. Along the way, Jo reminded Elizabeth more than once that they'd entered Johnson County. As the wife of a Sheridan County sheriff, this was to be noted and respected.

Grass licked the edges of the driveway. A backhoe sided a feed shed with a single bulb lit over its door. Strands of festival lights ran from the shed to a massive barn and back. Across the yard, the two-story house was lit from floor to ceiling. A trio of horses leaned against the railing of a corral. Their heads turned toward the car as they considered their newest guests.

Jo appraised the buildings, silent, her hands on the steering wheel.

"You all right?" Elizabeth itched to begin the setup. Guests were on the way, and she needed appetizers prepped and placed, drinks mixed and ready.

"Yeah," Jo said. "Well, no." She stared through the windshield, as if uncertain where—or whether—to park. "Didn't recognize the address before. Prior owner, though. The one I knew. And I haven't been inside."

Elizabeth watched the corner of Jo's right eye begin to twitch. "If you're sure you're all right…" It was uncharacteristic of Jo to remain close-lipped about much. At the moment, the woman was stiff, as though ruffled by a ghost from her past.

"Right as rain," Jo said, and nodded once, as though to convince herself. She twisted in her seat to regard Elizabeth. "Let's get to it."

Before Elizabeth could ask anything else, Jo was out of the car. Elizabeth stumbled out of the passenger side, then paused to adjust her costume. The fabric rode up around her middle, and she shimmied to shift the bulk.

Jo lifted an arm draped in purple satin. "I look like a bed sheet lost a fight with a bordello curtain."

"Remind me to murder my brother the minute he feels better. Of course, he would sign me up for Vesta." Elizabeth wrenched open the rear door to the SUV. She released the seatbelt that secured one box of stacked trays. With one knee, she boosted the box farther up into her arms and surveyed the yard.

A speaker pumped music through the barn windows. Classic rock spilled from the openings. Elizabeth calculated the distance to the house and eyed adding another layer to her load.

Jo lifted a crate from the cargo area. "If you can set aside the vestal virgins part, your gown of flames is pretty cool. I have to make do with a glorified grape necklace and an olive wreath."

"Holding all that wine, you definitely look the part of Bacchus."

"I'll try to act the part but maybe not fully embrace it until I'm home tonight. Feet up. Speaking of this wine, where are we setting up shop?"

"Casey's notes said that while the party will take place in the barn"—Elizabeth gestured with one elbow—"we should do any preparation in the house. Apparently, there's limited electricity in the barn and no plumbing."

"New owner must have had different plans..." Jo said under her breath.

Elizabeth studied her friend. "This is my official check-in with the god of wine and pleasure—you sure you are up to this? I appreciate that you jumped in to help as per usual, but you seem...off."

Jo met Elizabeth's eyes and nodded. "Show me where to set this down, and I'll be fine and dandy. Promise."

4

"Oh. I see."

"Yeah." Jo reclined against the kitchen counter, her wrists braced on the edge. After they'd unloaded some of their supplies, Jo had told Elizabeth about the previous summer. How she'd followed her gut to identify a murderer. "Another day in the life of a sheriff's wife, I suppose."

Elizabeth gave her friend a hug. "So this used to be his place." She shuddered, then continued, a hand on Jo's shoulder. "Casey owes you something fierce for coming back here. As do I."

"Nah, I'm happy to help, and I can already see changes to the property. It's a pretty little spread. Glad the place is in someone else's hands. Can't wait to find out who took it on."

When they'd knocked on the front door, no one answered. A sliding glass door on the wide deck stood open a few inches. A water dish and rope toy waited near a welcome mat. Elizabeth saw a breakfast nook, a kitchen, and the living room beyond through the glass. After a second round of knocking, they broached the entrance. Elizabeth slid the door farther open with one foot. She and Jo set their first load on the tile counters of the galley kitchen.

Custom cabinets lined the kitchen walls and gleaming hardware. Two of the cabinets yawned open, their doors propped against a dishwasher. The scent of wood stain waned in the air. A giant basket on the countertop held a half dozen apples. Their waxy surfaces shone under the lights. A painted dish of succulents sat on the windowsill, a ceramic cattle skull nestled among them. Two coolers blocked the doorway to the rest of the house. Above their heads, the sounds of a shower came to an end.

Elizabeth called out. "Hello! We're here for the catering. We'll wait in the kitchen."

The shower stopped. A muffled reply came from overhead. Elizabeth shrugged at Jo and the two began to lift the wrapped appetizer trays from the box.

Jo consulted a mammoth oven, its gas range topped with a vent hood. "Should I preheat the oven? There are a lot of buttons on this model. Might take a minute."

"Let's start at three seventy-five. We can always kick it up if we need to."

"Roger that," Jo said.

Elizabeth consulted her list. They'd need more of the items out in the car but those could wait. She didn't want to leave without talking with the host. Their first job was only a stroke of bad luck away from utter failure. "We'll need to serve in rounds," Elizabeth said. She consulted the items they'd unpacked. "Let's start with the mushrooms and crostini in round one, the smoked trout and dates in round two. Then we can figure out the rest of the timing. Casey said there are phases to these parties. Like when they learn clues about each other. We should time things so people will want refills on food and drinks."

Jo wedged some of the fabric of her costume under one arm. She reached over the sink for the liquid soap pump. "Lemon-lavender scented. How civilized."

"We'll ask the host if there's anything special we need to do. Maybe there's an art to catering a proper murder." Elizabeth pictured detective cloaks, monocles, and cigars in hand. A chalk outline on the floor, arms and legs splayed. Long debates, late into the night.

"You haven't been to one of these before? I've always wanted to host one. Clint said it sounded too close to his day job."

Elizabeth shook her head. "Seems a little silly. People running around in costumes, flinging accusations."

"What's wrong with the mythical deities? Besides, it's fun. You get to take on a personna, act out a part. I did a family reunion one and let me tell you, the sweet, gingerbread-baking grandmother character was anything but. Knitting needles one heck of a weapon. The games have all kinds of themes, like a sports event or a 1950's sock hop."

"I'm a brewer," Elizabeth shrugged. "I could get into a prohibition theme."

Jo dried her hands on a tea towel slung over a hook. "Oooh, flapper dresses and snazzy suits? Vintage cars and speakeasy energy—I love it. Count me in!"

"Maybe I could host when I get my own place. Have a housewarming party." Elizabeth tried to picture her own future place, a fuzzy image of that future vague in her mind.

Casey said they could live at Cloud Nine as long as they wanted. Still, Elizabeth had picked up and started over to chart her own destiny. She couldn't second guess herself now.

"Gin cocktails and canapés. Sequins and big band music." Jo did a brief Charleston across the wooden floor.

Elizabeth glanced out the window toward the barn. "Tell you what. I sure won't host it in a place without utilities. What kind of person throws a party with no toilets and Christmas lights?"

A voice Elizabeth recognized like a favorite sweater came from over her shoulder.

"Uh, this guy?"

5

A man in a skin-tight outfit filled the doorway. He wore a spandex top straight off the flight deck of the starship Enterprise. The corded muscles of his triceps bulged under the stretchy fabric. An upside-down, V-shaped pin completed the outfit. He'd darkened his brows into mountain shapes. Elizabeth spotted false, pointy ears poking out from his thick, dark hair. Like a space elf. He turned a tight circle, showing off the extent of his costume. While she stared, he crossed his arms, mirth in his eyes.

Kade Michaels.

Scores of butterflies took flight in Elizabeth's stomach. She willed her flippant comments back into her mouth, but they had a life of their own.

"The Roman Empire ended in 476 AD. It's doubtful any of their gods made it to space."

Kade broke into a grin. "I never pegged you for a Trekkie."

Jo volleyed her gaze from Elizabeth to Kade and back again. She took the empty platter from Elizabeth's hands and turned to fill it with vegetables from a plastic container. A smile played at her lips.

"Two boring summers at my aunt and uncle's house. Data's my favorite."

"I should have guessed."

Elizabeth's ability to spout trivia with little provocation was a telltale sign of her discomfort. Like a reflex, it happened most when confronted with a tense situation. Finding herself in the kitchen of a man whose presence turned her insides to liquid was a qualifying moment. "You do make a convincing Vulcan."

"At your service," Kade said, and bowed. "Thanks for coming all the way out here. This all looks great. I get that this isn't the typical setup, but Casey seemed to think it would work out. The kitchen is yours to do whatever you need. Out in the barn, I set up a bar area, and the tables are already set. How can I help you get sorted?"

By tanning my brother's hide for not telling me it was your party, Elizabeth thought. She would deal with Casey later. For now, she had a vehicle full of food and drink to distribute. "We can find our way around the kitchen. Maybe give us a timeline of when you would like us to circulate with food? We've got the kegs in the back of the car, so we'll want to put those with the rest of the drinks."

"I'm on it. I've got a hand truck in the barn." Kade moved closer to peek into the box.

Elizabeth could smell his soap, a woodsy scent of pine. When he stepped back and left her to the safety of her personal space, she wished him back.

"Looks tasty. As for timing, you can't go wrong. We do have some natural breaks in the game, but food throughout is great. I'll haul the kegs."

Elizabeth had lived in the area for less than a year and yet Kade had been a part of her story since she'd arrived. Their hot-cold energy had led to one night with a bottle of wine and their memories. Elizabeth savored the memory of that night like a memento on a mantlepiece. Then life got complicated, and they'd decided to focus on their kids, her son and his nephew.

They'd become like ships in the night. Elizabeth had stopped herself from attaching to the idea that she and this man could be a couple. Could build a life together. Kade was a businessman and had turned profits into a beautiful spread on the prairie. She was a broke teacher crashing at her brother's house. The gulf between herself and his life widened. She wished his attention didn't keep her up at night.

"Thanks," Elizabeth said. "That was Casey's task, but he's home. Or should be."

"Sick as a dog," Jo said to Kade. "I'm the replacement. He said this is some kind of murder mystery party?"

"Well, more like an employee-client appreciation party. But yeah, we thought a theme might be fun. Shake up the typical small talk a little. Get people to mingle."

"Sounds fun," Jo said.

Kade shrugged. "I'm trying to be more...fun. My employees tell me I need to loosen up a bit. Do something other than work."

"Makes sense. They say half of everyone is unhappy at work."

"Not all bosses put in the effort," Jo said. "Reminds me of camp in the summers. The head counselor took us all out for ice cream sundaes each year. We loved it. Almost made up for the crummy food and boiling hot showers."

Kade scratched at the back of his neck. "Oh, and I'm sorry about the utilities. I thought I'd have time to finish up the wiring at least. But, with the permit process and prepping for the car show, I ran out of time. At any rate, people will be in and out of the house to use the bathroom, but I doubt they'll be underfoot in the kitchen. I hope the distance isn't a problem."

Jo held up the fitness tracker on her wrist. "I don't mind getting my steps in."

"We got some of the lights up, but part of the path is still a little dark. Aim for the buildings, and you'll be fine."

Elizabeth wanted to ask about his nephew Benny. He was her former student but had moved schools. She was curious how he fared in his new classroom. She was about to venture a question when the whoosh of the sliding door signaled a newcomer.

"Kade, hon, I've got a generator out there running, but I think the coolers will be fine to hold the ice. What do you think?"

The speaker breezed in, more skin showing than not. She wore a white leotard that left no unanswered questions, a diaphanous cloak of snowy tulle pinned at her shoulders with large, gold grape leaves and white cowgirl boots. She held a bottle of fruity liqueur in each hand and pressed a cell phone to her side with her elbow. Without other pockets, Elizabeth couldn't fault her for lack of a different placement.

The woman evaluated the addition of Elizabeth and Jo. "Oh, help is here. Great." She handed Elizabeth the bottles.

"Liz, Jo, this is my neighbor—"

The woman extended a manicured hand, nails a sparkling silver. "Just call me Venus. And you are?"

"Bacchus," Jo said. "I'm wearing someone else's costume."

The woman nodded in acknowledgement of the purple satin, then turned to Elizabeth. She scrunched her nose as she took in Elizabeth's costume. "And you are?"

"Vesta. Goddess of the hearth."

"And the virgins, right?" The woman laughed and slapped her thigh. She patted Elizabeth's shoulder. "Don't worry. No one ever believes that part of the myth."

Gold glitter was scattered across the woman's plunging cleavage. She wore false eyelashes that gave her the look of a made-up macaw. The woman was fit, her thighs muscled, triceps carved. Elizabeth noted a smudge of lipstick on the woman's teeth, then licked her own in case. *Don't be petty.* "Nice to meet you," Elizabeth said, a tight grin plastered across her face.

"Okay, Becky—I mean, *Venus,*" Kade said. "I'll get the kegs, and then I'll meet you in the barn. We'll figure out the sound system."

"I'll be waiting," said the woman. She gave Kade a little wave and sashayed out of the room, as though aware that every pair of eyes watched her leave.

"Friend of yours?" Elizabeth asked Kade, despite not wanting the answer.

"Former employee, actually. Used to do my books, then landed a chiropractor turned horse breeder for a husband. Widowed now, poor woman."

Poor woman, indeed.

Kade continued, "Lost a son overseas. She's helping me out again at the shop. Going back to school to learn a trade and needed the money. We share a fence line, and I think she just misses company."

Elizabeth wondered what else they might share.

6

Gouda next to cheddar, brie next to feta. Elizabeth separated each type of cheese with a grape leaf. She nestled some of the roasted nuts and grapes among the piles. Preparation kept her distracted, her attention on the creation of a beautiful spread. The more she focused on perfection, the less she could stew on the conversation with Kade.

Through the window, she watched one car arrive and then a second. Guests unfolded themselves from the confines of their vehicles. They'd exchange hugs or handshakes and head for the barn. Costumes ranged from toga wraps to a man in a mermaid costume, wielding a trident. *Neptune,* she guessed.

She hadn't seen Venus a.k.a. Becky since the kitchen run-in, but Kade continued to greet people at the barn doors. Drink in one hand, he'd throw his arm around each newcomer and usher them inside.

"I know exactly what you're thinking over there," said Jo. She'd been filling finger bowls with pitted olives and cherries. "Throwing yourself a pity party is so last year."

Elizabeth crammed half a box of toothpicks into a tiny holder. She tucked it into the pile of soft cubes of Monterey Jack. She stabbed a few of the tiny bamboo skewers into the cheese. "I was simply admiring the costumes." She continued to peer through the glass.

In the driveway, new guests climbed out of a giant pickup truck. Each wore a sheet wrapped around themselves, toga-style. One wore sandals, but the other wore running shoes with knee-high socks. Each wore a crown of plastic greenery. Elizabeth watched the pair proceed to the barn.

"You could just tell him, you know."

"Tell him what?"

Jo smiled. "That you like him, what else?"

"There's no way that is happening." Elizabeth shook her head. She slid a stack of crackers onto another platter and then opened a second box. Night air sifted in through the still-cracked screen door. Crickets chirped and moths circled the porch light. "I'd be mortified. What if he blows me off? What if he acts like he has no idea what I'm talking about?"

"Pick up that gorgeous tray of cheese, carry it out there, and use it as an excuse to tell that man you can't stop thinking about him. Then kiss him, long and hard, until you forget whatever it was that pumped the brakes on your relationship."

"Jo!" Elizabeth's mouth hung open. To hear her silent wishes spoken aloud shook her focus. Left her raw.

"What? If I have to watch you mope around all night, I'll go mad. You still like him. *Admit it.* Then let him know—and before that Venus woman sinks her claws into him. For all our sakes. I saw the way she all but threw herself his way. That woman has legs up to her neck. It's always the horse people."

"Horse people?"

Jo nodded. "They spend more time in the barn than anywhere else. More of a workout than anyone knows. Bet she has glutes of steel to match."

Elizabeth glared at her closest friend. She readied a retort. She planned to deny every word. Tell Jo she was off base and that, in fact, Kade existed only as a pit stop on the journey that was her life. But the lie refused to leave her lips. Platter of cheeses in one hand, she hefted the crackers in the other. "It's not that simple."

Jo slid the door to the deck along its tracks until Elizabeth had clearance to exit. "It is exactly that simple."

The warmth of the summer sun dissipated with the sunset. A slight breeze brushed Elizabeth's cheeks, and a shiver zinged up her spine. "What do you think the Romans wore when they got chilly?"

"A hot mechanic. Now scoot."

7

Elizabeth grumbled under her breath as she picked her way down the flagstone path. The broad stones led away from the house and toward the barn. Her ballet flats found purchase on the uneven walkway as she balanced the two platters. The toe of her right shoe was worn, grayish against the black leather. One foot and then another, she willed any latent clumsy genes to remain at bay.

The flagstones ended at the driveway, the earth soft below her soles. She navigated the patches of grass and gravel between her and the barn. A few steps into the open space and the night spread its blanket above her.

Hercules arched overhead, his constellation bright diamonds in the black velvet sky. This far from city lights, Elizabeth was smitten with the celestial landscape. Bright pinpricks, a smattering of planets, and a wash of Milky Way painted the nighttime canvas. She craned her neck to drink in the view. Elizabeth felt small, insignificant. Alone.

A new pickup truck eased itself alongside the growing row of cars, its lights striping the yard. For a moment, Elizabeth was blind to her surroundings. She blinked, a rapid reorientation. Several of Kade's mechanics tumbled out of the vehicle and made a beeline for the barn.

The night hers again, Elizabeth found new resolve. She took a deep breath and continued her path. Music grew louder and laughter filled the air. Near the side door of the barn, coolers offered cans and bottles. Two Blau Brewing kegs bathed in ice. A stack of solo cups rested atop a bench near the doors. In the upstairs windows, guests chatted and danced. Several people crowded onto the balcony, drinks in hand.

Elizabeth eyed the rickety set of stairs that snaked up one side of the barn. They disappeared near the wide opening of the hayloft. *Can't be that way,* she thought.

The moon, a waning sliver, inched over the barn roof. Faint moonlight cast weak shadows across the yard. Moths and midges dove in haphazard arcs underneath the yard light. Somewhere in the growing darkness, a horse stamped and whinnied.

Elizabeth savored the calm. Out here, she didn't need to put on a brave face. Mask her feelings. Inside, she would need to play the part of a competent caterer. One-time love interest turned casual acquaintance. A faint buzzing sound shook her from the solitude. A beetle zipped off in the night. She resolved to claim a place on Casey's back porch with her own beverage when this night was over.

Her arms having grown heavy carrying the load, Elizabeth vowed to make it through the night. She straightened her shoulders and lifted her chin. *Focus on the job, feelings later.*

Light spilled from the south end of the barn near the coolers. Two guests, one in puffed out swirls of gray and brown with a big red splotch, the other inside a space suit, maneuvered awkward costumes over to the kegs. *Jupiter and Apollo,* she thought.

Elizabeth aimed for the entrance, hopeful for a door left open. Forty feet from the building, the buzzing sound returned. Platters in hand, she rotated to put the barn at her back and scanned the sky. Among the bright bulbs from the light strands, a small, blinking red light hovered near the house. The craft sped around the cars parked along the driveway. It dipped in and around the vehicles as though seeking occupants. For a moment, it zipped under the yard light long enough for Elizabeth to catch a glimpse of its form. Black and the width of a dinner plate, it looked like a child's toy, a helicopter with all the extra propellers. It flew the length of the roofline and then disappeared over the side. Her neck craned upward, Elizabeth almost dropped the food when a voice came out of the dark.

"Hey—are you lost?"

8

Jo approached, the crate on her hip. A selection of small bowls filled with the toasted nuts and pitted olives jostled inside. She'd placed a folded tablecloth on top to protect the contents.

"You all but scared me out of my skin." Elizabeth turned her gaze back to the sky, seeking the machine. "Ever seen one of those drones out here? The little ones."

"Those glorified remote control kids' toys? Clint can't stand those things. They have a heck of a time dealing with complaints. People are always flying them places they shouldn't, cameras and all. You wouldn't believe how many get shot down in the middle of town."

"People shoot them?"

Jo arched an eyebrow. "Liz, consider where you live. Can you think of a single person here who'd be fine with an electronic mosquito up in their business? Let alone taking live footage."

Elizabeth searched the darkness for the return of the blinking red light. The idea of a mobilized spy network unnerved her. A chill went up her spine at the memory of what it was to be stalked. Observed. "Guess not. Then why chance flying them over other people's spaces?"

"That's the thing about risk. It's a judgment call with a potential payout in mind." Jo shifted her load to the other hip and set off for the barn. "You ready to face the crowd? We've got ten minutes before the mushrooms are ready, according to my list. Time to get this party started."

Elizabeth followed Jo to the barn, her ears tuned in to the night's symphony. Crickets chirped and a horse whinnied. The rumble of a motorcycle faded into the distance.

She considered mentioning the drone sighting to Kade. Let him know one was poking around. An oversized, motorized insect. *If I get another chance to talk to him,* she thought.

Casey's mailbox often held catalogs carrying drones. Advertised alongside milking machines, goat vitamins, and horse tack, as an innovation. Drones were the latest tool for a rancher to keep an eye on their livestock. Handy for the ability to cover distances, the devices needed only proper piloting. Casey installed lights and cameras and called that good. Surveillance was not what his goat operation needed.

At the big barn doors, the women hesitated. A staircase of rough-hewn wood scaled upward to a large loft. From their vantage point, guests circulated, chatted. At the base of the stairs an old door straddled two sawhorses. On the makeshift tabletop was a magic marker, a stack of name tags, and the direction for each guest to get their set of clues from Vulcan.

Jo rested the crate on the door. She removed one of the bowls of nuts from under the cloth and set it next to a tiny vase of prairie roses. "Better," she said. "Inviting."

Elizabeth looked up at the party and sighed. "I'm going to murder Casey."

"No, you aren't. Not only would I have to turn you in, which would pain me, but he wouldn't deserve it. I know why you are still down here like a scared little mouse. It's the same reason you've been moping around the last several months."

"But—"

"Liz, I am this close to regretting helping you if this is what I'll have to deal with all night. Jo Wolf is a born helper, darn it. Open up to him. If you truly care for the man—or think you might—have the decency to tell him, once and for all. Drop the picture of the perfect time and place. That's the stuff of fairytales." Jo started up the stairs, not waiting for a response.

Elizabeth frowned and mounted the stairs to catch up. "You really think I'm after perfection? We can't all be like you and Clint. That kind of fairytale doesn't happen for most of us."

Jo stopped, mid-step. Elizabeth watched her shoulders tighten as Jo tipped her head side to side to crack her neck. She turned to face Elizabeth, a slow movement. Jo blinked a few times before speaking. "Am I to understand you consider that empty cradle of ours a storybook ending?"

Without another word, Jo stomped up the rest of the stairs and disappeared over the landing.

Elizabeth bit her lower lip as shame washed over her like a flood. Jo was one of her biggest fans. The woman who would move mountains for Elizabeth's family. In return, Elizabeth sent an arrow straight through her friend's heart. "Jo, wait. I'm so sorry!"

Regretting her comments, Elizabeth mounted the steps in quick succession. Near the top, she caught the toe of her shoe on the last landing. The newbie caterer—and her wares—were launched into the room.

9

Three things happened at once.

Several crackers tumbled to the floor and crumbled upon impact.

A pair of arms wrapped around Elizabeth as she fell into the chest of her rescuer.

From somewhere nearby, Jo said, "I'll take those." The platter, which still contained most of its contents, was whisked from Elizabeth's hands.

For her part, Elizabeth couldn't bear to straighten, though she knew she must. Without a mirror, she knew her ears had flushed bright pink. Mortification flooded her bloodstream.

Her cheek wasn't pressed against a random party guest. It was pressed against a spandex-tight, bright blue material. She squeezed her eyes shut.

"Whoa there," Kade said. He took hold of her shoulders and stood her up. "Easy on the steps. Reminds me, I need to sand them down a bit. You okay?"

"An average of twelve thousand people die falling down stairs each year," Elizabeth said. "Not sure about falling up, though." She avoided his eye contact as she stepped away from his embrace. She brushed imaginary dust off her slacks, then crouched to scoop up the cracker debris.

Kade knelt down to help. "Jo gave me the menu rundown. Looks great. I'm waiting on a couple more people to show up before we get started. Want the quick tour? Things will get busy once we start. I'd love to show you the place, raw as it is."

"Uh, sure." Crumbs collected, Elizabeth searched for a trash can, her hand out in front of her.

Kade held both hands out to her together, palms up. "No sense in wasting food. I'll take those. Let's give them to the chickens."

Elizabeth tipped the cracker bits into his hands. Several fine white lines scarred the flesh of his palm. A callus punctuated the base of two fingers.

Before Elizabeth could let Jo know, Kade headed for an exit near the end of the loft. She followed behind as he wove through guests clustered on benches and in camping chairs.

Elizabeth recognized a resident or two among the crowd. All wore costumes. She thought she saw a Hercules, fake biceps stuffed into a shirt. Another mechanic she recognized from Kade's shop was a convincing Cupid, a child's archery set slung over one shoulder. *A little too convincing,* she thought as she eyed the boxer shorts-turned-outfit.

Cupid caught her eye. He lifted the bow in the air and winked at her. Elizabeth frowned and turned her attention back to Kade.

"Who are all these people?" The question had the flavor of judgment. "I mean, I don't recognize many of them."

"Your car is in the shop often enough, you ought to know everyone by now."

Elizabeth furrowed her brow. She was unsure if the comment was a dig, meant to wound. Her hatchback was among the few belongings she'd brought from her old life in Seattle. At this point, its place in the driveway was as much sentimental as it was financial. As much as a new car would save her in shop costs, it would decimate her salary in payments. "Very funny. Must be the shift in dress code."

They'd stepped outdoors onto a wraparound balcony. Kade pointed at a spot on the boards. "Watch your step. It's a bit rickety there. Won't be for long, though. I have plans." He held his hands out over the railing and dusted them off into the darkness. A faint cluck from below signaled the location of the chicken coop.

Elizabeth stepped around the spot as Kade made a right along the backside of the loft. The balcony continued, a walkway wrapping around the barn. To their left, Elizabeth spotted the set of stairs she hadn't wanted to risk from the driveway. If she'd braved them earlier, she wouldn't have tripped. Wouldn't have the current urge to bury her head in the sand. He kept a quick pace, and she hurried after him.

Kade stopped along the backside of the barn. A weak moonbeam gave his skin an eerie glow as he faced the empty grasslands. He waved one arm in a sweeping arc. "This. This right here. Couple hundred acres. Creek runs through it. Not too many boulders. Lots of cottonwoods." His laundry list of features brought a smile to his face.

Elizabeth peered out into the moonlit landscape. The vast nothing promised freedom, privacy, and a little mystery. "Sounds like you made a good choice."

"That I did," he said. He started out into the night and was quiet for a moment. "A bit of a steal, to be honest. One man's loss and all that. Hard not to feel a little guilty, though. And the commute is a bit longer."

"Jo is happy for you, but this place gives her the creeps. She told me what happened last year. Awful frightening. Makes me love that donkey of hers even more. Did you know him?"

Kade dropped his brows, as if he considered what to tell her. With a slight tilt of his chin, he brushed a casual veil over the question. "No, I didn't know him. Might have been a customer at some point but we've got lots of those coming through on occasion. Jo cracked that case–the hard way. "

Elizabeth shivered despite the gentle summer evening warmth. "Had I known that, I wouldn't have asked—"

"She wouldn't have come if she didn't want to," Kade said. He stopped her guilt trip with a hand on her forearm. "I've changed things around, cleared out a lot of muck, and I think a place can be decent again, no matter its past. Don't you?"

"It is a great spot," Elizabeth said, unsure of the right response. She would consider how to approach Jo later. Starting with an apology. "I mean, at least from what I can see. Can't blame you for jumping at the opportunity."

"This lighting doesn't do it justice. Though I've been on a full moon ride, and the landscape is haunting." Kade paused, studied his shoes for a moment, and then looked up at Liz. "You should come sometime."

"I..." Elizabeth could hear Jo in her head, urging her to say yes. Say something. She gave a slight shake. "Moonlight is forty thousand times weaker than sunlight. Not I'd be able to appreciate it properly in the dark."

"Maybe a daytime ride then?"

"Oh, uh...sure," Elizabeth stammered. "I'd love to see Benny. What does he think of this place?" Elizabeth scrambled to regain her footing in the conversation.

"He loves it," Kade said over his shoulder. "Spends every minute he can out in the yard. Most of the time, he's got that microscope you gave him. Always bringing me a new kind of grass or dragging me over to see some bug. I can hardly get him indoors long enough for a bath and a meal or two."

Elizabeth grinned. Like her son, Benny loved nature. He was a quick learner and school was easy. As his teacher, she'd worked to get him new challenges that met his needs. When tragedy struck his family, he had to move in with his uncle and switch schools. Kade was devoted to his nephew, rearranging his life in every way to support the little boy. Elizabeth missed her former student but knew he was in the best hands.

"I'm happy to hear that," she said.

"He isn't here, or he'd want to say hi," Kade said. "He's actually staying at Marg's."

"Marg Hart?"

"Yeah," Kade said, and shrugged. "Since people will be in and out of the house all night, I didn't want him woken up. She offered."

They'd walked the length of the building. He paused at the hayloft in front of them, and Elizabeth stopped a few feet from where he waited. "Oh, no. I'm calling that bluff. You know as well as I do that Marg is nothing close to casual. What was her agenda?"

Margery Hart was a widowed horse breeder and cattle rancher with a sprawling, successful business and no direct heirs. Liz had dated her son before his tragic death. She'd learned about what prairie women can endure from the ranch owner. Marg did nothing by accident.

When Elizabeth peered at Kade, she regretted prying. A shadow crossed his face. She noted in the twitch of a muscle in his jaw that he didn't like having his decision second-guessed. *Well, too bad, Mr. Business Owner. This doesn't add up.*

Kade opened his mouth, then closed it again. He inhaled through his nose and then spoke. "She contacted me a few months ago. You know her style. Said she was sitting on money that needed to go to

Benny. Said his aunt would have wanted it that way and that since his mother couldn't...can't..." Here, he clammed up, nodded a few times, then continued. "She told me the money would go to him the complicated way or the easy way and that I could have a say in the easy way. Invited me over for drinks. Randall had the paperwork ready to go."

"Randall makes a mean Old Fashioned." Randall was Margery Hart's assistant. A few decades younger than the wizened woman, he'd been employed as her trusted sidekick for decades.

"That he does. Two of those and I agreed to a hefty college fund, a horse whenever he's ready for one, and visits to the ranch."

"Wow, she really worked you over."

Kade pressed his hands together and squeezed. "In truth, I'm grateful. She's a tough old bird and a good influence on Benny. I want him to have strong women in his life. On top of that, the fact that she can provide an inheritance is more than I could have hoped to do. Even in my best year at the shop." Kade turned away from her to step into the loft.

Elizabeth followed. She was about to sing her own praises of Margery Hart, when his eyes went wide, and he grabbed her for the second time.

"Watch out!"

10

Elizabeth's right foot dangled over empty space. Thanks to Kade, her left foot was still on the floorboards. He'd snagged her hand a second before she would have stepped through empty space and fallen to the ground.

"Oh, wow," Elizabeth said, trembling. She pulled her dangling foot to join its mate and flattened herself to the wall.

The hay loft held several stacks of bales. A few hay forks hung on hooks against the wall. A pair of gloves lay on a windowsill. The room smelled of earth and summer, a heady scent.

"Easy there," Kade said. He gave her hand a squeeze before he let go. "There's no giant pile of hay waiting at the bottom like in the movies."

Elizabeth's heart pounded in her chest as she attempted to regain calm. Was it the near fall or the proximity to Kade that had her on edge? "Why do you have a huge hole where people walk?"

Kade gestured to the nearby bales and rakes. "It's a hayloft. The hay is stored up here until you need it down there." He pointed to the hole. "You use the tools to toss it down when you need it. Most people don't dive for the opening."

"I didn't—"

Kade grimaced. "You almost did."

"Someone is going to get killed if you're up here feeding animals in the dark."

"Lucky for me, the horses are already bedded down for the night. You okay to climb down the ladder? If not, we'll go back around."

"Are you willing to spot me?" Elizabeth was thankful for the cover of darkness. This interaction was everything she'd tried to forget about Kade. She'd allow herself this flirtation before it was back to business.

"Third time's a charm," he said. Kade winked, then started down the ladder.

Before she ventured toward the ladder, she spotted a slim slice of light through the wall. Through the gap, she saw party-goers. Flashes of costumes, overstayed hair, and the low hum of a group. Snippets of their conversation filtered in through the gap.

"When do we start playing?"

"I hope I'm the murderer!"

"This beer is amazing. Where's it from?"

Elizabeth called toward the ladder. "Why does your barn have a squint?"

The ladder vibrated from its climber. Kade's head popped back up over the edge. He followed her gaze to the wall. "A what?"

"A squint. From medieval castles, back in the day. You can usually find them up high, somewhere there's a good view of the great room. Kings used them to spy on their people. Figure out who was loyal and who was a liar." Elizabeth placed her ear to the wall to listen.

"You can tell all that from a hole in the wall?" Kade climbed back up into the loft and crab-walked to her side. "What are people saying?"

"Shh." Elizabeth made room for Kade to join her. "Listen."

He pressed his cheek to the wall, his face inches from hers. He smiled a nefarious grin as he listened to the din. She caught the hint of mint on his breath.

"Anyone seen Kade? Maybe he's the murderer."

"Can't Thor kill anyone he wants with that fancy hammer?"

"How do we know when the person died? Like is there a sign?"

"I'm going to need more drinks for this."

"Huh. Never saw that before. Here's hoping I won't need to question the loyalty of my subjects anytime soon. You ready to rejoin the revelry, milady?" Kade gave a low bow with a sweep of his arm before he descended the ladder once more.

Elizabeth turned to follow him. Before she ventured toward the rungs, she put her ear to the gap one more time.

"So, is Kade single or what?"

11

Kade made Elizabeth promise not to fall again for the rest of the night before he left to talk with the guests. She shrugged off his concern, but on the inside, she was nothing but butterflies.

Elizabeth found Jo arranging appetizer plates on a low side table. Jo nodded a greeting before she returned to fanning out the napkins. Elizabeth wanted to relay every word of her conversation with Kade, ask Jo what it all meant. But when she met the pinched irritation across Jo's brow, she remembered the stairs. The cutting remarks she'd told her dearest friend. An apology was overdue.

"I'm a terrible person," Elizabeth began. "What I said was careless and immature. I know you and Clint have gone through hard times together. Incredible heartache. Honestly, I look up to you both. I want a relationship like you have—that is my goal. Instead of thanking you for being an example for how to be, I let my own drama overtake any sense I may have, and my mouth ran with that. I'm sorry, and I hope you'll forgive me."

"You aren't terrible," Jo said.

"Thank you."

"But—" Jo raised her pointer finger into the air for emphasis. She looked over Elizabeth's shoulder, then twisted to check over her own until she was certain of their relative privacy. "Your pent-up thirst for that man is driving uncool behavior, and I'm done hearing about it. I wouldn't be a good friend if I didn't hold up this metaphorical mirror for you. If you want to try to be together, do it. If you don't want to, then it's time to let that idea go and move on. If a situation with a man isn't inspiring you to be your best self, then he isn't the man for you."

Elizabeth bit her lower lip, willing the urge to comment to disappear. Moments like this were the least appropriate for an offhand fact, a distracting statistic. Her discomfort with the truth was not Jo's problem. She grabbed the ice pick from the table to stab at the hunk of ice in the bucket. After a few effective jabs, she set the pick back in the bucket and turned to Jo.

"I hear you. And you're right. I have been acting like a fool. Changing my mind so much I can't keep up with my own emotions. I thought I knew what I wanted. Knew who he was. Who I was. Then everything became so layered, and I let myself get caught up in that."

"No relationship is ever going to be perfect," Jo said. "And how fair is that even to expect of someone?"

"It isn't." Elizabeth thought about her marriage to Nick. It had been so easy to point to the cheating, drinking, and lying as the main causes of their divorce. These were valid reasons. At the same time, she'd declined attending the architectural awards and avoided his office parties. She'd stopped asking him about his hopes and dreams. She told herself she didn't want to meet any of his mistresses, face the other wives. But in truth, she'd resented his happiness at work. Elizabeth had put so much of her ambitions aside to have a son and care for him. She didn't regret that, but she hadn't advocated for her own balance. To admit that she'd contributed, even in a small way, to the downfall of their marriage was a bitter pill to swallow. "Relationships are hard."

"Truer words were never spoken. Now, we'd better get our ducks in a row. Looks like the murder mystery is about to start." Jo passed a platter of warm mushrooms to Elizabeth and picked up her own tray of crostini.

"Attention, everyone, we're about to start!" Kade perched atop a folding chair at the edge of the room. Becky clutched a handful of pens by his side. "Thank you all for coming—and wearing name tags." The guests chuckled at Kade's remark. A few slapped their chests where a name tag should be. "I admit I'm not up to speed on Roman mythology, so every hint helps."

Jo tilted her head toward Elizabeth to whisper. "Are any of us?"

Elizabeth whispered back. "I might remember a few."

She'd guessed the identity of most of the characters without reliance on name tags. The older couple was a Jupiter and Juno pair. The man wore the striped shirt he'd stuffed, Santa Claus-style, on which she'd noticed the giant spot. His wife had pinned a calendar page to her mint green jumpsuit. She wore a trio of plastic tulips tucked into her hair. Another man wore several dozen belts of all designs around his middle—a colorful Saturn. Minerva would be the person in an owl costume, and there was Neptune with his trident. He'd speared several strawberries from the buffet on the tines of his trident.

Around the room, guests had their mobile phones out, snapping pictures with each other. *If the Roman gods were real,* Elizabeth thought, *they would have been very into selfies.*

"You should have greeted each other in character and shared the gossip listed on your intro cards."

Elizabeth nudged Jo with her elbow and whispered, "Ooh, Kade's organized."

"I noticed," Jo said. "Good thing I'm a married woman or I'd be a goner."

"Now, I'm about to hand out the clues for round one," Kade continued. He held up a handful of folded cardstock pieces. "In this round, you'll learn more secrets and try to keep your own hidden. Venus will bring you a pen if you want to keep track of who's who. I suggest we all take notes." He buzzed from guest to guest, passing out directions and answering questions.

Thor called out from his perch on a stool. "When does someone die?" The guests laughed.

Cupid joined the sport. "Come on, we can't have anyone die yet. I'm on my first beer." More laughter filled the rafters of the loft.

Kade's cheeks reddened. "No one dies in the first round. We need time to get to know each other. Consider motives. We'll spend about a half hour in this round. The murder doesn't happen until the second round."

Cupid accepted his card from Kade, then asked, "How will I know if I'm dead?"

Kade huffed. "The victim's card will be labeled. You'll know if you're dead."

"I think Vulcan is hoping the victim is Cupid," Thor said. The crowd laughed as Kade rolled his eyes.

Elizabeth didn't recognize every guest, but the playful banter signaled the newest mechanics at the garage.

The gathering of characters, drink or snack in one hand, clues in the other, began to mingle. Soon, they'd paired off or stood in threes, exchanging clues. "That's our cue," Elizabeth said.

"We've got about fifteen minutes before the next oven timer goes off," Jo said. "Meet you in the kitchen in a quarter hour?"

Elizabeth gave Jo a thumbs up and offered her plate to a trio of guests deep in shop talk.

"All I'm saying," Thor continued, "is that they don't make glove boxes like they used to. Give me a '57 Cadillac Eldorado. They fit a whole cocktail set in that one. Nowadays, you can barely squeeze in the owner's manual and some fast food napkins."

"Speaking of napkins," Apollo said, taking one of the small cocktail squares from Elizabeth. He eyed the stuffed dates before selecting a plump one. "What's in these beauties?"

Along with his space suit, the man wore a halo of pointy cardboard, gilded with spray paint. He'd painted a homemade necklace of plastic horse figurines to match. *Rhett would approve,* Elizabeth mused. "Mostly chèvre. My brother makes it fresh."

"Wrapped in prosciutto and drizzled with honey, I see." Apollo popped one in his mouth. "Divine."

"Any nuts inside?" Thor waved a hand over the parcels, hovering over the plumpest date.

"These, yes. Almonds." When Thor made a face, Elizabeth was quick to continue her list. "But we've got mushrooms out, and bruschetta. My homemade corn nuts, too. Those are on the drink table."

"Corn nuts. Great bar food, but I never understood that name," Apollo said. "It's not like they're real nuts."

Thor shook his head and waved a hand in the air. "Not touching 'em. They're nut-adjacent."

Apollo rolled his eyes. He confided in Elizabeth. "Don't take it personally," he whispered, loud enough for Thor to overhear. "My friend here is more of the oat-milk-and-avocado-toast type. Allergies out the wazoo."

Thor socked Apollo in the arm of his space suit. Elizabeth gave them a half smile and moved on.

Other groups took turns reading from their cards. They'd pause long enough to take a snack from the tray before they returned to character analysis.

Their small talk was tedious for Elizabeth. She waited, impatient, for another opportunity to talk with Kade. She was determined to say something. To do something. Jo was right. It needed to be now or never so life could move on. Nerves or not, Elizabeth knew she had to take action. Kicking herself for doing nothing would end tonight.

As she meandered between the guests, offering food, looking for a chance to chat with Kade, she caught snips of their conversation. Many took to their roles with the commitment of a professional thespian.

"Jupiter, Jupiter, Jupiter. Why are we always doing what that guy says? If only a new god would claim the throne."

"Everything is a fight to Minerva. She was born in armor and all. I don't trust her one bit."

"Keep an eye on Diana. She brought a full quiver, if you know what I mean."

"Thor is sporting new sandals. Wonder if he paid for them..."

"Janus is so two-faced. You never know the truth in what he says."

Elizabeth stifled giggles at the game design. To someone who knew their Roman deities, there were many clever comments. Was she the only one who appreciated the writing?

She ducked around Hercules and Apollo as the pair argued over who was stronger. Apollo reached out to snag a snack before she passed.

Behind them, Kade and Becky stood in close conversation.

"You have nothing to worry about," Becky said. "I'm here now. I never should have left in the first place, and here you are, saving me all over again." She lifted onto the balls of her feet, lips pursed, as if to plant a kiss on Kade's cheek. Kade spotted Elizabeth and stepped back from his neighbor.

What was this? Elizabeth froze, mouth open, considering the scene. Sure, Kade had seemed into her, but she was a one-guy kind of woman. *What if he wasn't a one-woman kind of guy?*

"Elizabeth. Hi. Uh, do you need me to change a keg?" Kade's cheeks retained their flush. He held eye contact with Elizabeth and avoided Becky's glare.

"Nope," Elizabeth said. "I think I'm needed...someplace." She turned her back on the couple and made a beeline for fresh air.

12

In the kitchen, Elizabeth tossed one baking sheet onto another waiting in the sink. For extra clatter, she flung the spatulas onto the pile. She cranked on the tap for the hot water. Elizabeth scrubbed at the dishes until her hands were bright pink. No matter what she did, the words still played in her mind, on repeat.

Jo was right. Elizabeth had waited too long, banked on Kade hanging around until she was ready. If she was ever ready.

And now, he was all but in the clutches of someone else, with others waiting in the wings. Elizabeth rinsed her hopes down the drain with the pan scrapings.

Elizabeth muttered to herself as she dried the pans and tucked them away. "Goddess of love *indeed*."

"What was that?"

Neptune, with his flowing beard and mermaid's tail, ducked his head into the kitchen.

"Oh. Hey, Raj," Liz said. "I didn't know I wasn't alone. Don't mind me. Talking to myself."

Raj worked at Kade's Garage. A top mechanic, he managed the garage when Kade was gone, his second in command. Together, Elizabeth and Raj studied her own car's ailments many an afternoon. He always tried to find the most cost-effective solution to her car troubles while she bemoaned the aging machine. Raj had even been instrumental in teaching Leia, Elizabeth's dog, new tricks.

"No worries," Raj said as a smile played across his lips. "Dishes make me angry, too."

Elizabeth liked the mechanic. Raj was detailed, yet kind. He was warm when Kade verged on gruff. She could see Raj owning a shop of his own one day. "You caught me in a moment of self pity, that's all. I try to keep it more together in public."

"Hey, your secret is my secret." Raj adjusted his mermaid tail to align with his rash guard top. The tail was a sheath of shimmery fabric with the tail fin sewed onto the bottom.

"Cool costume," Elizabeth said. She removed a set of tubs from the refrigerator and stopped to look him up and down. "You've got King Triton vibes going on."

Raj laughed. "Thanks, I think. Yours isn't too bad either."

Elizabeth looked down at her robes. She'd knotted the hemline at her shins, a trick that made walking easier—and safer. In the kitchen, she'd donned an apron to protect the satin fabric from stains. "I'm a bit of a modern version, I suppose. I would have rather dressed the part of Trivia, but Casey picked our characters."

"Where is your brother—off decorating a fabulous house somewhere?"

"Sick," Elizabeth said. "Jo rescued me. She's helping me tonight. Otherwise, I'd be running around serving like a chicken with my head cut off. Speaking of serving, who are all these people? Lots of folks in there I don't know. At least not in costumes."

"Employees and their wives or boyfriends and such, if they have them. Our newest apprentices from the college. Some of our biggest clients, the repeat customers. Kade wanted to celebrate the garage, this place. And he didn't want to do it alone."

"I've heard of the apprentice program. That must be rewarding."

She offered the plate of fresh-smoked salmon stacks to Raj. He selected one and took a bite. "We coach them up right before our busiest time of year. Teach them everything from working on cars to handling important customers with kid gloves. They are ready for summer. Like the car show. We hire the best of the lot, and they stay on to train the next year's cohort. The rest get great experience and a solid letter of recommendation." Raj took another bite and chewed, thoughtful. He swallowed. "Most of them."

"Sounds like a win for everyone."

He nodded. "Working with greenhorns takes serious effort. No matter what business you are in. Kade made them my responsibility which I both appreciate and loathe in equal parts."

Elizabeth cracked a smile. "Kind of exciting, getting a fresh batch. At least, that's one thing I love about teaching. While I adore each year's group of kids, meeting new young people is often the fresh start I forgot I needed."

"I'm from California. I've had enough excitement to last me two lifetimes. I prefer life on the quieter side."

"Last time I was at your place of business, it seemed anything but quiet."

Raj grinned. "True. But I'll take the rumble of an engine over an office full of coworkers any day. Cars, you can work on, fix. Repair the parts that break. Make them new again."

Elizabeth macerated a cup of blackberries with a pestle. She poured the crushed fruit into a jug of lemonade. "I can see that. Sometimes it felt like no matter what I did, I couldn't save every kid. Their environment, my lack of resources, you name it. You can't just take out the hurt or the neglect, replace it with joy. People don't work that way."

Raj nodded. "I'm working on a car right now. Special order. The customer had me take out the rumble seat from a classic bootlegger and turn it into a trunk. Couldn't save the upholstery and they wanted the storage space. It took everything I had not to freak right out. Might as well put in subwoofers while I'm at it."

"Rumble seat?"

"Like a jumpseat. You flip it up when you need it, fold it down when you don't. It's a bit of a safety issue now." Raj flicked to a picture on his phone and held it out to Elizabeth.

Cherry red paint, red wheel covers. "Beautiful," she said, not knowing how else to compliment a car.

"It will be, when I'm finished. Almost there. I'm waiting on a couple knobs. Can't find them anywhere. The darn thing flaps open when they hit a bump. The inside was a mess when we got it. Left out in the sun. Split leather, stains everywhere. Busted locks. It's a shame when people don't take care of what they have."

Jo ducked in the kitchen and picked up the plate of salmon appetizers. "Better put the mushrooms in and prep the next tray of cheese. People are into this whole motive-seeking business, and it's getting ugly in there. Ceres accused Diana of peeking at her clue card. Janus is overly appreciative of the Olympus Porter, and Saturn is passing out his rings like leis."

"Let me get the doors for you," Raj said, and followed Jo out.

13

Elizabeth piped a tight swirl of goat cheese mousse on each slice of cucumber. She opened the plastic container of thyme leaves and topped each round with a sprig. She alternated cucumbers with the apple and cheddar stacks. The pattern created a checkerboard of temptations.

While Casey was the family chef, Elizabeth was catching up. She loved the preparation and the outcome. Whether the repetitive, measured tasks or the precision of creation, the movements soothed her. Gave her hands an occupation so her mind could think.

Now, Elizabeth allowed her thoughts to drift to Kade. What she'd heard through the crack. Seen in the loft. Or thought she saw. The scene of intimacy played itself on repeat in her thoughts. She shook her head as if to dislodge their hold. Had the interaction been two-way?

It wasn't as if she'd held a silent, solitary torch for Kade. There'd been her crush on Corbin, the owner of a local animal rescue. A momentary distraction. He'd since reunited with an old flame, leaving Elizabeth alone again. After the sting of rejection, she'd picked up her feelings and moved forward.

Elizabeth had hesitated to believe in her feelings for Kade. Second-guessed his and her own ability to be a partner, and now he might be with someone else. Here she was, paying the price in Kade's kitchen.

Alone for the moment, she allowed herself a chance to study her surroundings. *His* surroundings. Newer, stainless steel appliances, a tiled backsplash in neutral colors. Cheery yellow walls. Pictures of Benny covered the fridge. Fishing on the creek, holding up a school award, handsome in his Christmas sweater. Four cookbooks stacked on a shelf, a bowling trophy on top. Coffee pot, tea kettle, and spices near the stove. Succulents in the windowsill, an apron on a hook with *You name it, I'll grill it* printed across the front. It was the kitchen of a decent man. One with whom Elizabeth may have lost her chance.

"Is it safe to enter?"

Elizabeth glanced up as Kade peeked in from the hallway. "The kitchen is open."

Kade had an empty tray under one arm. "Jo said to scoot my idle tail out here and help carry. As a general rule, I obey her orders."

A jumble of complicated emotions crossed Elizabeth's mind as she stumbled over a reply. "Yeah, me too." *Smooth.*

"What can I carry? Tension is building out there, and I know I stress eat when I'm under pressure."

"Who died?"

"That's coming up. I gave everyone a ten-minute break until round two. I'm to be useful, as Jo put it."

Elizabeth regarded her work in progress, then opened the refrigerator for inspection. "How about I send you out with more hummus? I've got the veggies cut. Let me get another bowl." She rummaged among the containers on a shelf.

"Between you and me, I kind of hope I'm the victim," Kade said.

Elizabeth withdrew a box of pre-cut celery sticks. She gave them to Kade. When her hand brushed his, she felt a zing of warmth. *No,* she told herself. *Stop it now.* "Why do you say that?"

"Murder mysteries are hard work." He tucked the celery under his arm. "There are so many details to track. Notes to take. People to scrutinize. If I'm dead, I can spend the rest of the time refilling platters."

Elizabeth handed him a second tub of chopped vegetables. "Well, you can start with the carrots," she said.

A giant, furry blur bounded in from the hallway and crashed into the back of Kade's knees. With a loud bark, the dog announced his presence to anyone who'd missed the entrance.

Kade laughed and bent down to scratch between the dog's ears. "Hi, boy." He looked up at Elizabeth. "You said the magic word."

"Please? I don't remember saying that."

Kade set the food back on the counter and patted his shirt with both hands. Sixty pounds of husky raised up to press both paws to Kade's chest. The dog licked his owner's face. "Nooooo. The C word."

Elizabeth rewound their conversation. "C-A-R-R-O-T-S?"

Kade nodded and reached for the container. "Mind if I..."

Elizabeth shrugged. "It's your party." She watched as Kade extracted a carrot stick and held it in front of the dog.

The animal did an immediate about face. He sat, a perfect statue, and watched the treat. Kade used hand gestures to run the dog through sit, down, and play dead. Then he put the carrot stick in one hand and hid both hands behind his back. "Brutus, where's the carrot?" The dog nosed an elbow. When Kade revealed the empty palm, the dog nosed the opposite elbow. Kade gave him the carrot and another round of pats.

"His name is...Brutus?" A fact bubbled up in Elizabeth's brain, a detail she needed to remember. "How long have you had him?"

"New Year's present to myself," Kade said. "Adopted him from Corbin. His owner died. Now, he's part of our family."

The memory surfaced, a dark history. "Winton Black's dog?"

Kade nodded. "Corbin worked with him some. Made sure he was going to be okay. I was worried about Benny. Turns out, they are the best of friends."

"That's how Rhett is with Leia. She won't leave his side." Brutus sniffed at Elizabeth's hand, and she stroked his sleek fur. "I've heard good things about you, Brutus." The previous winter when his owner had been pushed over a cliff to his death, Brutus had refused to leave the body of Winton Black, loyal to the end.

"Maybe we should get them together for a playdate."

Elizabeth looked at Kade, her brow knitted in confusion. "Rhett and Benny...or Leia and Brutus?" *Or Elizabeth and Kade?*

"All of the above," Kade said, and met her eyes.

"I'd like that." Clear in her head, Elizabeth could hear Jo's voice as though she were standing next to her. *Drop the idea of a perfect time and place. Tell him how you feel.*

Kade watched her, silent. His was the intense gaze of a person waiting for a specific response. Elizabeth remembered the intimacy of his moment with Becky. Sure, she'd made some distance between the two of them the last few months, but it wasn't like he was banging on her door. Maybe he was busy with someone else but that didn't work out so now he was interested. *What if he's a jerk like Nick?*

Elizabeth's resolve crumbled. How could she declare herself to someone whose motives she questioned? She resorted to her coping strategy. "Brutus seems incredibly loyal from all I've heard. So is Leia, and they were sled mates. You know, the Chukchi believe that two huskies guard the gates of heaven."

"I did not know that." Kade crossed his arms, a hint of a frown touching his lips.

Elizabeth's words spilled from her mouth, a mortifying gush of nerves. "The guardians won't let anyone in who hasn't been kind to dogs."

Kade uncrossed his arms and stepped closer to her, searching her eyes. He reached out a hand to stroke her cheekbone, a soft brush of his skin against hers. "Elizabeth Blau, you are something else."

"What does that mean?" The heat from his body warmed hers as the air between them electrified.

He took another step closer. "Am I the only one of us who was there for that kiss last fall?"

Elizabeth wound back her memory clock. As though it was yesterday, she could picture them both back on Casey's couch. The bottle of red. His lips on hers. The feeling of someone listening to her, wanting to hear what she said. Then liking what he heard. She remembered. *Okay, Liz, here's the time, here's the place. Tell him.*

"Liz," he said, inches from her now. She wanted to reach up and trace the crows' feet at the corners of his eyes. Run her fingers through his hair. Instead, Kade put his hand on her forearm to draw her close, a feather-like touch. "What happened to that date you promised me?"

The spell snapped. "The one you kept putting off? Last I remember, that ball was in your court. A girl will only reschedule so many times before getting the message she's low on the scale of importance."

Kade's hand dropped to his side, and he took a step back. "Come on. You know things were complicated back then."

The slide of the patio door in its tracks interrupted their conversation. Becky walked past the kitchen, saw the two of them from the hallway, and stopped. The woman plastered on her biggest smile. "Just little old me. Too many glasses of that lemonade. Might have added a little something to it, if you know what I mean." Her giggle became a snort and she covered her mouth. "A girl can only take so many accusations, after all. Janus blamed me for Jupiter flirting with me, and Minerva said I was after celestial real estate. I swear, Kade, some of these folks are taking this game to a new level."

"Sounds intense," Elizabeth said. She gave Becky a weak smile. "Pardon me. You're in front of the food."

Becky flashed a glare in Elizabeth's direction and stepped to the side. She moved toward the door, then turned back. She extended a hand to squeeze Kade's forearm. "You don't mind if I use the one off your bedroom, do you? I left my makeup bag up there." Before he could answer, Becky winked at Elizabeth and headed upstairs. The creak of her footsteps above was audible in the otherwise quiet house.

"Complicated. *Uh huh.* Right. I get it now." Elizabeth picked up the vegetable containers and another package of cocktail napkins. She refused to look him in the eye. Would not dare let him know how close she'd been to believing him. A fat, hot tear slid down one cheek.

He blocked the doorway with his bulk. "Please, let me explain. She's just a—"

"Excuse me. I've got a job to finish."

Kade pressed his lips together and stepped aside. With her elbow, she opened the sliding door, not daring to look back.

Brutus bounded out of the dark and onto the porch. He barked at Elizabeth, and she clutched her armful closer to her chest. One container fell to the ground, and Elizabeth backed up to the wall. Her pulse raced as the frantic dog's yelps echoed in the night.

Kade burst outside. Brutus focused his energy toward his owner. Quick, sharp barks, an urgent alert.

"Hey, hey. Brutus. No. Stop. What is it?"

Brutus hopped off the porch, barking outside the bright ring of porch light.

"Are you okay?" Kade tossed the dropped celery in the trash. "I don't know what's gotten into him. What is it, Brutus?"

The dog started toward the barn, inserting a howl between barks. He doubled back and again ran up on the porch to Kade to continue the alarm.

Elizabeth peered into the dark. The yard was empty, the row of cars quiet. Laughter and conversation spilled from the barn's loft windows, but other than the incessant barking, the night was quiet. "You first," she said to Kade.

Kade stepped out onto the path, and she followed close to his elbow. Brutus had rankled her remaining sense of calm. Elizabeth still reeled from the conversation with Kade, her emotions on edge.

Twenty feet out, at the place where the house lights and festival lights failed in their effect, a figure lay across the path. Fish scales shimmered in the moonlight.

Raj lay face down in the grass, Neptune's trident lodged firmly in his back.

14

Red and blue lights flashed in the window above the kitchen sink. Elizabeth soaped, rinsed, and dried the same dishes twice as she stared into the distance. Officers swarmed the yard, the barn. They came in and out of the house, talking into their radios and among themselves. She cleaned up as best she could without crossing the crime scene tape.

Brutus was shut into an upstairs bedroom. His plaintive howls could be heard by anyone in a two-mile radius.

"This is the last of it," Jo said. She unpacked the crate she'd carried in from the barn, setting more serving pieces next to the sink. "I gave my statement. Once we get these sorted, we are clear to go home. We'll need an escort out of that parking jam, though. I don't know about you, but I'd like to make that as soon as possible."

The minutes after Elizabeth and Kade found Raj had blurred in a reactive frenzy. Kade had rushed to Raj's side, tears streaking his face. He checked vitals, shouted to Raj that they would get help. Elizabeth's hands shook as she pulled out her phone to dial 911. She tried to speak to the operator, but her voice shook, and she struggled to form sentences. They'd remained, planted, until emergency personnel arrived.

Now, shaken from the horror, she wanted answers. "You were with Raj right before this happened. What did he say to you?"

Jo shook her head. "Not much. He followed me across the yard. We talked about parties, being a wallflower. We passed Kade on our way to the barn, and I told him you'd be coming behind me with more food. Kade said he'd help you. When we got to the barn, Raj held the door for me but didn't come inside. Said he needed to go back and visit the little boys' room before Round Two started."

"That explains why he came into the house in the first place. We started talking, but then you came, and he got distracted." *If I'd only kept talking to him—or cut him off— he might be here, still, playing the game.*

"I see what you're doing in that head of yours, Elizabeth Blau. You can stop that right now. No way are you taking on the guilt of that poor man getting stabbed."

Elizabeth paused, letting the warm water flow over her hands to rinse a plate. "But I..."

"No buts. This is in the hands of the officers, now. They'll find out what happened and make sure justice is served."

"I'd feel better if Clint was one of them," Elizabeth said. Sheriff Wolf was one of the best in the state, according to the shiny new plaque on his desk. He wasn't among those gathered in the yard, though, as he'd taken on babysitter duties for Elizabeth.

"Me, too," Jo said. The dust had settled after the helicopter left, Raj inside in critical condition.

Elizabeth stacked trays into a box alongside serving utensils. "Who would do such a thing? And to attack him in the dark like that."

"It's terrifying," Jo said. She'd shared her own story of an attack earlier that evening. The ranger had her alone, leveraged surprise. If not for the heroics of one stubborn goat, Jo would no longer be with them. Her lip quivered. "To overpower a man and then..." She shuddered.

Again, the imagery stole Elizabeth's focus. She had to get out of there, get some space. "Okay. I've cleaned all I could. What will we do with this leftover food?"

"Ask Kade, I suppose." Jo shrugged. "It's his home."

15

Elizabeth found Kade in the living room. He'd sunk into the couch, head clutched in his hands. A cup of cold coffee sat, untouched, on the side table. Blotchy stains smattered his shirt. Elizabeth wouldn't think too long on those.

"Hey," Elizabeth said. She paused near a black and white photograph of a windswept grassland.

Kade lifted his head. "Hey."

"Jo and I finished our clean up. We'll put leftovers in the fridge. Unless you'd rather we do something else?"

Kade groaned and put his head back into his hands. "Anywhere is fine. I'll take it to work or..." He trailed off, reconsidering. "Leave it wherever. I'll figure it out."

Elizabeth studied the man in front of her, broken and grieving. Two hours ago, they'd been in the kitchen together. Then again, so had Raj.

"I'm so sorry. If there's anything we can do..."

"Thank you," Kade said. His eyes were bloodshot, the eyebrow penciling smeared onto his forehead. He wrapped his arms around his knees as though to cocoon himself into a place of protection. "I've been drowning in my own sorrow, and I forgot that you were there. That you saw him, too. Like that. How are you holding up?"

"I'm okay," she said, a lie. She couldn't shake the images of Raj impaled, the horror on Kade's face. Wouldn't be able to erase them anytime soon. Then she thought of Kade's experience. "I'll be okay. Jo and I will take off so you can get some peace."

Kade nodded and looked away.

In the kitchen, Jo waited with the last crate balanced on one hip, keys in hand. "Ready?"

In the driveway, a few official vehicles remained. Officials spoke in low voices, took measurements. As the women loaded their equipment into the car, Elizabeth ran through the night's events. There'd been mere minutes between when Raj left Jo at the barn and when they'd found him. Whomever stabbed him hadn't been far off. Been there among them, at the party.

"I'll be right back," she told Jo.

"Where are you going?"

"To snag a picture of that guest list."

16

The trident was a nice touch, if I do say so myself.

Completely unplanned, I have to admit, but what do they say about taking the bull by the horns?

Not that this guy was a bull, by any means. More like a docile heifer.

Some people are too nice for their own good. It's always "how are you" this, and "have a wonderful day" that. Makes me sick to think about it. It's like there's no room for you to be having a bad day. Obnoxious, really, to pretend that there's nothing ugly in the world, that it will all work out for everyone. Sometimes people talk to you as though if only they are positive enough, it will wipe away any of your problems. Ridiculous.

If that was a thing, I would have talked my way into a different life a long time ago.

Poor guy.

Tonight, I learned that puncture wounds to the chest cavity don't cause a ton of blood. At least not like on television. Not that I could see. Not if you leave the weapon where you lodge it.

Boss said to get the job done, silence him. I did that. Couldn't use a gun. Too loud and messy. "Bring a knife"—so I did. Aim for the heart. Losing lung capacity restricts breathing. Can't yell. Can't beg for mercy. Immediate quiet.

In an ideal situation, I prefer other weapons. Distanced, reliable. I'd been watching for the opportunity all night. Turns out, I needed to seize the moment. It was too perfect a set up. The great thing about the trident—other than death by a sea king's staff in a landlocked state—is that thing had everyone's handprints on it. He passed that thing around the party like it was an Oscar statuette. He was so proud of the craftsmanship. Like anyone else wouldn't have thought to spray paint a garden fork silver. Those poor excuses for law enforcement out here will run the prints and find all of us on the handle. Even me.

Still, they have to try. Won't that be fun?

They interviewed each of the guests before we could leave. No, I didn't see anything. No, I don't know anyone who would want to do him harm. No, I can't think of any way he could have stabbed himself in the back. Yes, you can contact me anytime with further questions.

Fools.

They're probably still there, standing around their patrol cars, debating whether it was an attack or if he somehow tripped and fell on the thing in the dark. They'll find alcohol in his system. It was a party, after all.

We all saw him there.

I'd been watching him for weeks, waiting for an opportunity. Had to figure out how much he knew, what he understood. Try to get him to trust me. Tell me things. Learn what he'd done with the secret he wasn't supposed to know.

But I also had to watch him when no one was looking. Let's face it. All of us act one way when people are around and another when we are all alone.

The problem with secrets is that they exist in levels. If certain secrets get out, feelings might get hurt. Others get out and marriages end, politicians get ousted, and businesses fail. If you find yourself on the wrong side of a secret you can't be trusted to keep, the situation gets delicate. Intense. People have to be called. People like me. I was asked to step in, assess, report, and then act accordingly.

Can't let the decisions of one ruin things for the many.

No one was looking out for him in the end, and he was unprotected.

Too bad the gods and goddesses are nothing but a myth.

17

Bone weary, Elizabeth closed Rhett's bedroom door behind her with a soft click. She padded down the hallway to the living room. Jo sat slumped on the couch, her feet propped up on the coffee table, a wet rag across her forehead.

"Rhett's sound asleep," Elizabeth said. "Thank you again for lending me your spouse."

"Clint would've been just as happy to have a sleepover. The Wolf Den B&B is always open. Especially to adorable little boys and their well-behaved dogs."

Elizabeth opened a cupboard door and poked around for a serving dish. "I appreciate the two of you more than you'll ever know." She extracted a container of leftovers from the fridge and loaded the plate.

"Don't get all mushy on me now," Jo said. She bent over to pluck a design book from the table. She flipped through the glossy images. "I'm too tired to get up and hug you over it. My mother was a waitress on Route 66, a stop sign diner. I don't know how she stayed upright all day on her feet. One night of it and I'm going to need epsom salts and a foot rub when I get home."

Elizabeth crossed in front of the couch to set the plate on the table. She scooted the stack of her brother's magazines and video game controllers out of the way. She plopped down on the cushions next to Jo with an audible sigh. "If you and Clint hadn't offered to kid-sit, we wouldn't have been able to book the event. Not to mention you covering for my wreck of a brother."

"Speaking of the wreck," said Jo, "where is he?"

"Snoring away. I could hear him through the door." Casey's hallway had a master suite on one side, a bathroom, laundry room, and the guest bedroom Elizabeth shared with Rhett on the other. It was cozy, but comfortable. When she'd packed up everything and left Seattle, it was a welcome haven. Keeping things small meant more savings for their future. "He left a note that he took some meds and hit the hay."

"Yuck. There isn't much worse than suffering through a tummy bug. One fundraising banquet, I ordered the crab. I kept reliving that bad decision the entire night. At one point, I remember Clint coming into the bathroom and covering me with a blanket." Jo took a bite of a carrot stick. "Slept on the tile that night, the bath mat rolled into a pillow."

"Too many of us have had that kind of night. He'll survive."

Jo reached for the wine bottle opener and uncorked the bottle of red. Elizabeth set two glasses next to the bottle. Jo filled each before handing one to Elizabeth.

"To our first event. It was nothing like what I pictured when I said yes to Casey's hair-brained idea, but it can only get better from here."

"A toast to the new business. May it be a long-lived venture for my favorite sibling duo." Jo clinked her glass against Elizabeth's, took a sip, then set her glass on a coaster. She nestled into the couch, pulling a throw blanket over her lap. "Now. Want to talk about the rest of the night?"

"I'm still reeling."

"While you were transferring Rhett to the car, I tried to pump my husband for information. His phone buzzed nonstop, but he remained tightlipped. That tells me so much more than he thinks it does. That means they still aren't willing to put whatever happened to paper."

"Do y'all have some kind of husband–wife privacy protocol?"

"We've found a rhythm over the years. He spares me much of the ugly and won't tell me anything that'll put me in danger."

"Seems like a solid plan."

Jo righted a tipped mushroom, then popped it in her mouth. "That said, we have misunderstandings. It's not like I can help overhearing him sometimes. In fact, there are certain things I'd pay good money to un-hear, if I could."

Elizabeth could only imagine what information Jo heard by proxy. Crimes, accidents, arguments. The hardest sides to being human.

Jo reached for her glass and took another sip. She plucked a second mushroom from the plate and took a bite.

"How are they? Other than lukewarm."

"Tastes like the forest. In a good way," Jo said. "I must confess I'm not a big fan of mushrooms. I try to put them in things whenever I can, though. All the health websites say we should be eating them in every way, shape, and form we can. Casey's goat cheese sure doesn't hurt."

"Anything living thing that is part animal, part plant is suspect." Elizabeth reached for one of the caps and sank her teeth into the creamy center. They'd mixed the cheese with herbs and sprinkled the tops with smoked salt before baking. The result was a burst of earthy flavor. Elizabeth reached for a second helping. "Ooh, these did turn out well."

"What is hard to swallow, still, is how close we were to Raj—before." Jo stared off into the distance, wine glass in hand. "We'd each seen him moments before it happened."

"That is the hardest part," Elizabeth said. "I keep thinking that if only there'd been the smallest delay in his movements, this wouldn't have happened. It also means that whoever did the deed was there. With us." She thought of the dark yard. Rows of cars along the gravel. The big barn full of people.

"You think it was one of the guests?"

Elizabeth reached for her purse, abandoned on a couch cushion. She rummaged inside the bag for her phone. "Wouldn't it have to be?"

"That's the thing about living way out here—people rarely come by on accident."

"But why would anyone be after Raj? Why tonight?" Elizabeth scrolled through the names, most of which she didn't recognize.

Jo finished her glass and poured a second. "Let's hope they found some clues. They'll be back in the morning for another look in the daylight. Kade will have to go over it all again."

Elizabeth nodded. "He was kind of in a daze in a corner by himself. Told him if we'd left anything we'd get it later. I didn't know what else to say."

"Poor man. Finding Raj like that was awful enough. Next week is the car show, and now he's down his best mechanic. I don't care who those new apprentices are, they are no Raj."

Tears slipped over Elizabeth's cheeks as she thought again of the man who'd trained her dog. Coached her in changing a tire. She suppressed a sob and searched for distraction. "Tell me more about this car show."

"It's a tradition. Local car club runs it. Turns out lots of our friends and neighbors, cooped up in garages all winter, like to work on old cars. Come summer, locals break out with every vintage vehicle imaginable. Cruise Main on Sundays. There are prizes for the best of categories. Anyone can enter, though certain people seem to have more time and money to get a car in top shape than others. You don't have to know about cars to know when you see a nice one."

"Sounds impressive."

"It is, even if you don't know much about cars. Fun, too. Vendors, food, the whole nine yards. It becomes an all day affair. I couldn't change a spark plug if you paid me, but I love seeing the classics shined up and pretty."

"Let me guess. Kade helps people get their vehicles show-ready?"

Jo swirled the wine in her glass. "They do serious business working on those cars throughout the year. Then they polish them up for the show. The biggest players take their vehicles all over, turn it into a business. Like flipping houses. You'll see everything from Prohibition coupes to amped up trucks with tires bigger than your kid. It's kind of fun to see the variety."

"Sounds like a great excuse to get outside. I'll put it on the calendar."

"You've survived your first Wyoming winter. You know the true value of our summertime."

Elizabeth wrestled a pack of cards from beneath the table. "Any chance you'd play a few hands? I don't think sleep is coming for me anytime soon."

"Deal me in."

18

Elizabeth slept a fitful night. She and Jo had played cards into the early hours until each was certain sleep would come. When Elizabeth roused herself from deep slumber the next morning, it took every effort to stand upright and shrug into her clothes. With a yawn, she dragged herself into the kitchen.

The rich smell of fresh coffee flooded Elizabeth's nostrils. Eggs sizzled in a cast iron pan on the range. Casey whistled *Old Man* as he poked at the omelet with a spatula. He added a handful of chopped veggies and a sprinkle of cheese.

Leia lounged in the middle of the kitchen floor. The dog kept her nose pointed toward the scent of temptation. More than one dropped tidbit taught her the value of sticking close to the chef. Rhett lay in the living room on his tummy, a spread of building blocks in front of him. He'd created a fortress into which he placed a few of his treasured animal figurines.

"Morning, you two," Elizabeth said, rubbing her face.

"Fresh pot," Casey said. "Grub will be up in two shakes."

"Thanks for getting Rhett up." Elizabeth reached for the coffee. She poured a full mug and added a splash of cream from the fridge. "I didn't even hear you come in."

His back to her, Casey replied, "Don't worry about it. I figured you'd had a hard night."

"Indeed." Elizabeth fetched a plastic donkey out from under the couch and passed it to Rhett. "I still appreciate it. Your night wasn't great, either. You must feel better this morning."

"Last night, I hydrated with a bowl full of Danny's homemade bone broth, about a gallon of ginger tea, and then I slept like a log. Kind of think I should do that most nights. I feel so darn good. Start a movement."

"Maybe skip the imported oysters step," Elizabeth said, "and go straight to hydration." She took a seat at the hightop stool behind the kitchen counter. "Coffee and breakfast is quite the treat."

"Purely selfish. You have to tell me everything as soon as that caffeine hits your veins. People keep texting me as though I was there, like I have a clue about what is going on."

"Where you were supposed to be, if I may remind you."

"It's not like I wanted to hug the toilet for the better part of the night." Casey set a plate in front of her. With a flick of his wrist, he slid an omelet out of the pan and onto her plate in a neat half-moon. He passed her a bottle of hot sauce and a bowl of cantaloupe cubes before prepping his own plate. "Now spill it before I go into detail about my suffering and ruin this perfect meal for both of us."

Elizabeth rolled her eyes before stabbing a forkful. "I'm sure you saw the news. It was terrifying. Still is." She gave Casey the rundown of the party, from arrival to dismissal by the Johnson County sheriff.

Casey shivered. "Attacked at a private party in the middle of nowhere. I don't know how they say the investigation is ongoing. Someone had it out for Raj."

"Raj was stabbed with his own trident."

"He was Poseidon?" Casey scooped some of the fruit onto his plate.

"Neptune. Roman gods, remember?"

Casey took his plate and mug to the couch and reached for a remote. "You know I can't keep any of them straight. I used the internet to figure out our costumes."

Elizabeth rotated her stool to face the living area. "There was talk of whether he tripped and fell backward somehow or if someone attacked him from behind."

"Let's hope daylight brought a little clarity."

19

Casey held the fermenter in place. Elizabeth opened the valve in the brew kettle to pour the cooled wort into the conical, steel container. The barn baked in the heat. The smell of animals and their feed permeated the walls.

Brewing had become a rhythm for the siblings. A time when they would team up to create something, together. Elizabeth was thankful for the simplicity of these times. The easy way she and her brother could exist, side by side. She prayed for their continued dedication to this new version of family. For Rhett's sake, yes. But also for the children she and Casey should have been allowed to be.

Elizabeth coached her brother through the brewing process. He took to it like a fish to water. From milking his goats, he understood the importance of sterilization, consistency, and temperature. Beer was a natural next step, and he practiced until he could brew a predictable product. Elizabeth had a bonafide assistant.

For now, they used a walled off room in the barn, but Casey had big dreams. Expanded distribution of his cheeses would allow him to add a small commercial kitchen. They were a few permits—and paying jobs—away from completion, but potential was ripe. For both of them.

Elizabeth added water to the five-gallon container. Before she could ask, Casey held out a fresh pack of yeast and a pair of scissors.

"Thanks," she said. "You read my mind."

"Nah, you're a good teacher."

Elizabeth sealed the container with the fermentation airlock. The device with its twist of tubing reminded her of her days as a chemistry teacher. While she'd adored the elementary students—their energy and joy was infectious—her heart was in high school. The district had yet to give her a formal offer for the fall, but Jo was confident it would be at Sheridan High.

"To be fair, I've never taught a minor how to make alcohol, but I'll take the compliment."

Elizabeth approached the upcoming school year with wary interest, regardless of assignment. There was a part of her that longed to take a different road. Away from the planning and grading and stress. One that led back to her hobby. She'd worked at a brewery to put herself through college. She missed the simplicity, the schedule, and even the clientele.

Patience, she told herself. *Life has a way of working out.*

"Twenty-four hours ago, I wasn't able to stand up, let alone help you." Casey stacked buckets in the corner and gathered their utensils to wash inside.

Elizabeth wiped her hands on her jeans and followed him to the house. Her tank top stuck to her back, her feet sweating inside her boots. "Your recovery is miraculous, given how you looked. Like death warmed over."

"You don't know the half of it. I don't want to detail the hours after I left you. Me and the mop are besties now."

"Ew. Could have done without the mental picture."

"You're welcome," Casey said, and made a brief bow. At the sink, he cranked on the blue handle to wash his hands. The scent of lavender filled the room as he sudsed himself from elbows to fingertips. "Aside from the awfulness, how was the rest of it?"

Elizabeth shook her head. "I can't set aside what I saw."

Casey dried his hands on a towel that hung from a wall hook. "I get that. I guess I'm wondering if you thought our plan would have worked out...if...well."

"You mean, aside from the visual of a giant fork sticking out of a man's back, did everyone have a good time?" Elizabeth opened the dishwasher to add the funnel, ladle, and glassware.

"Yeah. Basically."

Elizabeth sighed. "Hard to tell. Most is a blur. People were eating, drinking. Seemed to enjoy what we brought. Jo did most of the barn hosting while I prepped in the kitchen. We tried to match the rounds of the game they played the best we could." She didn't tell her brother about the one-on-one time with Kade.

"About that. Meant to give you more details ahead of time. It slipped my mind."

Elizabeth glared at her brother, and he grimaced in return. "Like the fact that it was at Kade's place to begin with?"

Casey winced. "Neglected to share that little detail as well."

"Neglected or left out on purpose?"

"So, how was it?"

"Don't give me that look."

"What look?"

"Like you're innocent. The one where you're trying not to smile. Like you've done something sneaky but somehow great and you're waiting for me to admit that."

Casey opened the refrigerator and selected two bottles. He let the door shut with a *thwup* and gave one to Elizabeth. He twisted off his cap, clinked the lip of his bottle against her unopened one, and took a long swig. "You mean the one where I know you secretly loved being there? That you like him. *Really* like him. Seems like you are the only one who won't admit that truth. Stone. Cold. Facts."

"All right, fine." Elizabeth crossed her arms. "*Yes,* I like him. There. I said it. There was a moment on this balcony thing that—"

Her brother raised both eyebrows. "I love this story already."

"It wasn't...well it was...It doesn't matter. The evening ended in a horrible tragedy."

"Completely true."

"And that will be all anyone remembers."

"So, I guess this referral for our next gig is a fluke?"

20

Elizabeth tapped the end of her pencil against a pad of paper as she considered their next booking. Casey explained they'd been hired to cater an opening at a tiny art gallery the day of the car show.

"Let me guess. Sweeping landscape paintings with cowboys on horseback in the distance or cowboys on horseback close up. The crowd won't know much about art but will want to look like they do. People wearing bedazzled jeans who own horses worth more than their cars."

"Honestly, Liz, it's like the last several months haven't taught you anything. People here have interests beyond livestock."

"Ah. So, it's those giant canvases on which someone splashed all their leftover acrylic paint. Now they want to charge people a grand to take home something Rhett could've made."

Casey laughed. "I think it's photography," he said. "I wasn't fully awake for the call. And lay off the stereotypes."

"Fair enough. What are the details?"

"This one should be pretty straightforward. Cheese pairings with wine and beer. Those nuts you made. Appetizers that we can set out and leave. Some kind of dessert. We'll have to come back and clean up, but we don't need to do any kind of service as people will be coming in and out. Mingling."

"Interesting timing, picking the same day as the car show."

"Actually, it's pretty spot on. The gallery is on Main, and there will be tons of foot traffic. Throw in a little food and they're guaranteed to draw a crowd."

"A strategy of sorts. Not that I have experience in art openings. One problem, though. What in the heck do we serve at an art gallery that makes sense with a car show?"

"Now that, dear sister, is our job to sort out."

Elizabeth puffed out her cheeks then pushed on one with the pencil eraser, emitting a puff of air. "What if we went with a picnic theme? Mini sandwiches and Petit fours. All finger food. I've got a decent recipe for tapenade if I can find it."

"Don't get too fancy," he said. "Remember the audience."

"So, it's back to bedazzled jeans." Before Casey could interject, she continued. "I'm going to run to the store. I need a few things and some ideas." She turned to Rhett. Her son had lined his plastic animals up by height, in descending order. The skunk was last, the brontosaurus first. "What do you say, Rhett? Do you want to come with Mommy to the store or stay here with Uncle Casey and..."

"Wash the dog. Leia was rolling in the corrals again," Casey said. Leia moaned from her spot on the tile and rolled over.

"Gross," Elizabeth said at the same time Rhett said, "Dog!"

Her son had taken his time talking. Rhett relied on a limited selection of single words and the occasional phrase. He was most talkative when the topic involved animals. They'd yet to find an animal he didn't want to see, name, and know.

She and Nick, Rhett's father, tried not to worry. They'd begun the slog of collecting opinions, options. Assurances came that it was too early to tell if his limited speech would remain a preference. Her former mother-in-law liked to float the idea of a diagnosis. While the teacher in Elizabeth was also curious, she hesitated to advocate for a final answer. Two years old was early in the game.

"I appreciate the honesty, buddy," Elizabeth said, and gave her son a kiss on the cheek.

21

One fat drop hit the pavement. Then another. Gray polka dots on the asphalt. Elizabeth considered her grocery list from the comfort of her car. They needed the regular items: milk, bananas, coffee. She'd also added cream cheese, cinnamon, and whole nutmeg. She had the urge to bake, to fill the house with tasty smells, and make a little less room for sadness.

Elizabeth's adventure to the grocery store was part errand, part research. She would seek inspiration among the aisles.

The late afternoon shower rolled over the mountain like a stampede. This rain shower was the front edge, the warning before the onslaught. Elizabeth grabbed for her wrinkled shopping bags and ran for the sliding doors. Her phone chirped from deep inside her purse, but Elizabeth waited until under the cover of the awning to check the ringing device.

Kade's Garage.

Dashing from her car to the front doors of the grocery store had left her out of breath. Elizabeth paused to slow her pulse before answering the call.

"I just made it to the store in my car, and I think we are both still in one piece. But call me next week, and I might have some business for you."

"This is not a business call."

Elizabeth worried she'd been too flippant. Too dismissive of the weight of the last twenty-four hours. She'd been careless. *How to recover?* "Oh?" *Smooth.*

"Benny's been up in his room all day reading. While I hate to discourage books, I'm fairly certain my role as guardian includes getting him some fresh air and adequate vitamin D. So, I was calling to see if maybe we could get the boys together. Dogs too. Heck, I could use some sunshine myself."

Elizabeth looked across the parking lot. The rain picked up as promised. Dark clouds, puddles, and ponds. Shoppers extended umbrellas over their carts to race for their cars. Others huddled outside the doors with Elizabeth, waiting for a break in the deluge. "Have you looked outside?"

"Oh, yeah. That. It's supposed to let up in an hour or so. What do you say we meet up at City Park?"

Elizabeth savored the sound of his voice. She waited for her nerves to kick in, the urge to take up quiet space with facts and distractions. Instead, she was calm. Her heart remained in her chest. She could get used to this. "Leia isn't too fond of a leash, but I think she'll make an exception for a social outing."

"Playground structure, three o'clock?"

"Great. Looking forward to it. Uh, Kade?" Elizabeth ventured a question before she could talk herself out of it. "How are you? If it's okay to ask."

Elizabeth heard the shuffling of the phone in his hand. The sound of a body sinking into a squeaky chair. She pictured him in his office, the tiny room sectioned off one end of the garage. Chock-full of filing cabinets and boxed car parts, there was little room for his six-foot frame.

Finally, he spoke. “I’m not great, but I’m here. Trying to put on a brave face for my crew. What’s left of it, anyway.”

Elizabeth wasn’t certain how to respond to this crack in his vulnerability. The confusion of emotions settled in her stomach like a rock.

22

At home, Elizabeth unpacked her list of items along with cherries, a cabbage, pork shoulder, shiitake mushrooms, and a package of frozen jackfruit.

Elizabeth pulled out a large bowl into which she shredded carrots. Next came the cabbage which she sliced into thin shavings. Mustard seed, apple cider vinegar, salt, and pepper. She tossed the mixture and set the bowl in the fridge.

She was knee-deep in slicing and pitting cherries when Casey and Rhett came in from the barn. Elizabeth held up her ruby-stained fingertips to her son, whose eyes went wide. Casey extracted a popsicle from the freezer and handed it to the little boy. Rhett slurped on the lime green treat. Leia watched, anticipating drips.

"Well, this looks exciting," Casey said. "But why jackfruit?"

"I went to the little health market. I assumed a vegetarian like yourself would approve."

"I do, in the general sense. What I don't get is what you plan to make."

"With checkered flags, hubcaps, and summertime the name of the day, I'm thinking of a picnic. We can make a big jug of berry lemonade for the non-drinkers. Do some fruit skewers. I can also do individual corn cakes and sliders with a cherry barbecue sauce and coleslaw. I'll make the traditional pork, but I want to experiment with mushrooms and jackfruit. See if I can get a vegan version."

"Hate to burst your creative bubble, but I'm not sure the place will be crawling with vegans."

"Maybe yes, maybe no, but I'd like to keep options on our menus. Each event is a chance for me to generate ideas. Practice pairings. I've never made burger buns, but I'll try. And I'll figure out gluten-free. We can put out a plate and see how it goes."

"And here I thought I was the only chef in the family. What's the rest of it for?"

"I promised Jo a batch of cinnamon rolls in appreciation for playing the part of my brother. You'd think she'd ease up on me given all that happened, but I got a text first thing this morning asking when she could expect delivery."

"Maybe she has news to trade for them."

23

Elizabeth removed pans from the oven. Each held a dozen rounds nestled against each other. The buns smelled of cinnamon and a hint of cloves. Their golden spirals steamed from their resting place upon vintage metal trivets.

Casey said, "Those smell like heaven."

Elizabeth ran her knife around the edges of each pan. One was a circle destined for an ornamental plate. She would bring this to Jo. The other was the standard rectangle, an old cake pan unearthed from within Casey's cabinets.

"Where did this pan come from?"

Casey gave her a weak smile. "It should look familiar. It's one of the few things I kept from our house. Back then. Took it with me in my pack."

"A cake pan?" Elizabeth scrutinized the dented metal, a standard issue.

"You may not remember, but Mom used to make us our birthday cakes. Most of them were standard chocolate or vanilla. But one time, she made you a strawberry version using a drink mix. Kind of gross. Anyway, Mom put serious effort into the decorations. She made all these little scenes with icing and candy."

Scenes from long-ago birthdays played in Elizabeth's mind. Scenes flitted through her memory. "Wasn't there an ocean one? I think I remember her using the plastic treasure chest from the fish tank."

Casey nodded and made a face. "I forgot about that part. We both lived, so she must have washed it first. She also turned gummy worms into seaweed. I remember getting blue frosting in my teeth from the waves."

"I wish we had pictures," Elizabeth said. The vintage ache settled in Elizabeth's chest, lodged in her heart. To have Casey cherish a happy memory was unusual.

"Might be some in a box somewhere," Casey said.

The reality that he'd retained and used something battered and beaten, a leftover from their childhood, was a surprise. The idea that there may be pictures from their past as children was incomprehensible. "I'd like to see some. One day."

"I've learned a little something in my advanced years—"

"Ha ha," Elizabeth said.

"You get to decide how life controls you," Casey said. "The story you tell. It's taking me some therapy and my own mistakes to understand that I choose what I take with me on my journey."

"Like packing a suitcase of memories."

Casey nodded. "Mom's cake pan is my way of laying claim to what I want from our history and letting the rest stay behind."

Elizabeth lifted the pan with matching potholders. She flipped it over to release the buns onto the cutting board. The pan was warm through the padded fabric. She turned it over to examine its dented backside. For her brother, this was his inheritance. A single tie to the past.

Elizabeth thought back to her hasty packing job all those months ago. She'd crammed her car full of the necessities she and Rhett would need for a new life. There wasn't room for more.

She sold the rest, in part for the gas money but also to free herself from attachment. Now, she wondered if she'd been too hasty to part with her memories. "What if we decide what to keep and what to toss out in moments when we are least prepared to make that decision?"

"When it comes to the past," Casey said, "I don't think you ever break free from it. Not really. But, you can choose how you carry it. Whether through an old leather jacket or a beat-up aluminum cake pan. Every new moment is a memory the next. We make those choices again and again."

24

Elizabeth slathered the tops of the now cooled rolls with maple cream cheese frosting. On the thrift store glass plate, her rolls looked picture-ready. Like something in a magazine. On impulse, Elizabeth snapped a picture. If their business was going anywhere, she needed to think like a marketer. Take more pictures.

The image of Raj sprawled on the ground again took over her thoughts. She closed her eyes and willed the nightmare from her mind.

Breathe. Elizabeth nestled the plate of rolls into a grocery bag on the table. From the other pan, she chose two rolls for a small plate. She cut one into several pieces before carrying the plate to her brother and Rhett.

Casey accepted the plate before Rhett could lunge for the treats. "Looks like pillows of heavenly calories."

"I'm going to run the other batch over to Jo. Thanks for keeping an eye on your nephew while I'm out."

"You mean thanks for cleaning him up after the epic mess he's about to make?"

"Yeah, something like that," Elizabeth said. "Consider it payment for the heaven that's about to hit your taste buds."

"Getting a little cocky, are we?" Casey held the roll up to his nose and inhaled. "Okay these do smell fantastic."

"Trying to think like a businesswoman. It's something I've always wanted, so I've got to play the part."

Casey offered Rhett one of the pieces. The little boy palmed the hunk of pastry and mashed the cream cheese end into his mouth. His eyes sparkled as he chewed a piece of the pillowy soft roll.

Minutes later, Elizabeth parked in the Wolfs' driveway. Buck and Bessie were in the corral, tails swishing. Each approached the bars to sniff at the arrival. "Sorry, guys," she said. "These treats are for your owner."

Elizabeth let herself in the side door. She kicked her shoes off at the mat and continued inside.

In the kitchen, she found Jo rifling through a drawer. Elizabeth set her bag on a chair. "Lose something?"

"I'm looking for that orange peeler. You know, that cheap orange plastic stick with a notch on the end? I swear those things have been around since my grandmother's age. Can't peel an orange without one."

"I brought your thank you," Elizabeth said.

"Almost worth it." Jo reached into the bag and extracted a roll. "Do you have time for tea?"

"Coffee?" Elizabeth took a seat at the breakfast table.

"It's old," Jo warned.

"So am I," Elizabeth said. "Or at least that's how I feel."

Jo laughed. "You've barely approached anything I'd call old, let alone gone over any hill. Where is this coming from?"

"Casey and I were talking about the past. About Mom and Dad."

"Oh?" Jo removed a mug from the rack of hooks above the coffee pot and poured from the carafe. She placed the mug on a coaster in front of Elizabeth. *Someone loves you in St. Louis* was printed across the ceramic.

"It was one of those conversations that sneak up on us when we least expect them. I don't know if Casey or I are equipped to talk about our past, let alone deal with it."

"Is anyone?" Jo wiped at the countertop with a sponge. "People spend many years and lots of money on figuring themselves out and still don't know how to talk about it."

"Not everyone has a mother in jail because she murdered their father in self-defense and a brother who disappeared for a decade."

Jo rummaged in the bag and then brought her own mug and a plate to the table. "I put my foot in that, didn't I?"

"In truth, you got me thinking. When you think you've escaped the past, it comes up and bites you in the tush. Usually when you least expect it."

"Ain't that the truth." Jo sank her teeth into a cinnamon roll and moaned in delight. "This ought to be criminal."

"I'll share the recipe."

"Nope, I prefer when you're indebted to me and therefore my personal chef. Plans for the rest of today?"

Elizabeth glanced out the window. She loved the view from Jo and Clint's house. It sat on a small bluff that overlooked a ravine. Acres of space stretched out toward the mountains. "Kade and I are taking the kids—and the dogs—to the park. In Buffalo."

"I knew it!"

Elizabeth faced Jo. "Knew what?"

"There was a spring in your step when you got here. You had no business being that way after what we went through unless something happened with Kade."

Elizabeth looked down at the mug she held in her lap. "Don't make me feel any more guilty. I'm already beating myself up about that. Did Clint find anything out?"

"Not his jurisdiction," said Jo. "Sheriffs respect county lines. The Johnson County wars may have happened a hundred and forty years ago, but that tradition is still going strong. We are relegated to the new cycle like everyone else."

A vibration rattled the inside of Elizabeth's purse. She fished out her phone and, for the second time, took the call. She showed the screen to Jo before answering.

"I'm sorry, I have to cancel," Kade said.

"Is everything okay?"

From across the table, Jo raised her eyebrows at Elizabeth.

"The deputies have been here all morning going through surveillance videos. They aren't done yet, so I won't have time to fetch Benny and Brutus."

"I understand," Elizabeth said. Though she didn't, not really. The elation she carried all afternoon began to leak from her like a punctured balloon. "Have they found something?"

"I'm not sure," said Kade. "Maybe. I'm really sorry, Liz."

"How about I come to you?"

25

It's true what they say, Elizabeth thought. *The way to a man's heart is through his stomach.*

Kade's moans of pleasure made his gratitude clear. Between bites, he offered her a place to sit, sweeping files off the stool in front of a computer terminal, but she declined. In one hand, he held the roll as icing dripped down his hand. The other held a thermos with Kade's Garage imprinted on the side.

"These are incredible. Enid has nothing on you." He licked the icing off his palm, Elizabeth watching his every move.

"Don't tell her that," Elizabeth said, her breath in her throat. "I'm a bit of a one trick pony. That woman has depth and breadth which I will never know."

"If Gary ever retires, you'd make a mean sous chef."

"A high compliment. If there's one thing I do know, it's how to make an espresso. Then again, I probably shouldn't work anywhere with free access to coffee. I'd be so jittery I wouldn't be able to interface with the public."

"I've had those days," Kade said. He stuffed the last chunk of roll into his mouth and chewed. "You didn't have to do this, but I'm grateful. That was probably my breakfast, lunch, and dinner. Today's docket is slammed, so I may inhale the others. I'll do my best to save one for Benny tonight."

She'd met Kade in the vestibule of his shop. The garage had five bays, a lot in the back, a tiny break room, a few chairs for customers, and Kade's cramped office. "Seems quiet," she said. "Is this typical for right before the car show?"

"We are officially behind, something I hate to admit. Do you happen to know a body detailer?"

"Not that I'm aware of. Unless this is a trick question and it's you."

"That's what I was afraid of. I'm going to be working some late nights if I can't find more mechanics. I reached out to the college to see if anyone is close. I'm going to have to call down to some of my buddies in Casper, see if anyone down there is available to come up and help. I can't do this without Raj." Kade sat atop a squat filing cabinet, arms crossed.

"What happened to everyone else?" Elizabeth glanced into the shop for signs of helpers. One pair of legs in coveralls stuck out from beneath a Cabriolet.

Kade held up one hand and counted off on each finger. "One is out for the week at his sister's wedding. Two apprentices took off after the murder and one is out sick. The one I've got left is doing the best she can with detailing for the show and all the regular business."

"Goodness," Elizabeth said. "I'm glad you have at least one left."

Legs scooted out from underneath the pale pink convertible, the rest of body followed atop a wheeled creeper.

"Hey, Liz."

26

Despite the smudges of grease, Elizabeth recognized the springy hair, glasses, and freckles. They belonged to a certain college student and part-time documentary filmmaker from Colorado who'd come to Elizabeth's rescue on New Year's Day.

"Alma?"

"Good to see you again. Little bit warmer this time of year." Alma smiled, a slim space between her front teeth. In boots and holding a wrench, hair tamed by a tied bandana, she looked the part of a modern day Rosie the Riveter.

"Glad to see you too. Summer break from the documentary degree?" Alma's videography skills helped them solve a mystery together. The woman's critical eye missed few details, and her journalistic nature knew which questions to ask.

"Ian went off to Hollywood. Got a job on a real set. I need cash to save up for my next piece, let alone graduate school."

"Forgive me for not pegging you for a mechanic."

"My dad and I worked on cars when I was a kid," she said. "I'm decent at the basics and picking up the rest, car by car. This way, I get decent pay and a chance to work on the Tardis."

"I didn't know you were into time travel," Elizabeth said.

Alma chuckled. "Dad was the *Dr. Who* fan." She pointed toward a bright blue muscle car in the parking lot. "Dad let me keep our project car. He's the original owner. Sixty-five Mustang and it's in better and better shape. Part of the benefits of working here. When we're off the clock, Kade lets us use the tools, and he gets the parts at a discount."

"Solid reasoning," Elizabeth said. She took a second look at Alma's car. Chrome reflections, a bright silver. Burgundy vinyl seats, fuzzy dice in the window. The license plate read TARDIS2. "I can see why you'd love that car. It's a charmer."

"I'm not the only one, either." Alma reached for a clean rag to wipe at her face and hands. "I get offers on it almost every day. One of the customers tells me if he has to keep seeing it in the lot, he'll have to steal it for himself. I'm fairly certain he's joking."

"Maybe keep your keys close by." Elizabeth recalled the half jokes cloaked in truth she heard as a female brewer. It wasn't everyone, but it was enough to notice.

"Kade says I have a knack for the work. Says I can turn it into something big. Have my own shop, if I stick with it."

"What about your film career?"

"I've got plans," Alma said. "I'm checking out graduate schools. Kade made it sound like I have a shot at a permanent position. If I can find something that works with that, I'm in business."

Kade nodded. "We've got a lot riding on the show going off without a hitch," he said. "I need mechanics to be a steady hand when things get busy, and with Raj gone..." He trailed off and looked away.

Elizabeth was curious how much energy he employed to hold it together today, to pretend he wasn't a wreck on the inside. The Kade she'd first met was all bluster and confidence. She'd grown to know this man, the version that would give everything and then some for the people in his life.

"I'm keeping up," Alma said. "I think. I'm quick, I'm clean, and I don't complain."

"And I appreciate you for it. Raj said you were our top recruit this year." No sooner had he said his former mechanic's name than Kade started to choke up. He bit his lip and looked away. "I need coffee. I'll make a pot for all of us. And I may need a second cinnamon roll to go with it."

27

Kade closed the office door and switched on a desktop fan. The device teetered on the desk, a rickety contraption. He reached for a giant water bottle and took a drink, eyes closed.

Two people jammed into the tiny office fit like sardines. Not wanting to stare at Kade, Elizabeth scanned the bays. She watched Alma slide back underneath the Chevy and spotted a bird's nest in the rafters.

Elizabeth said, "I like Alma. You're lucky to have her."

"Because she's a phenomenal mechanic or because she saved your life?"

Elizabeth looked at him. "She told you?"

"I had to squeeze it out of her. She was teasing me about you coming over. Something about my cheeks turning red." Kade peeked at Elizabeth. "I tried to tell her mechanics don't blush, but she refused to listen. She said for what it was worth, I have great taste because you are a brave and awesome woman. When I asked her why, she told me what happened with the sled race and Bobby coming after you."

The drama of the sled, the race, and her reckless choice to follow a murderer up a mountain on a snowmobile. She got lucky that day, and there wasn't a night she didn't get down on her knees in thanks. "She's no shrinking violet herself," Elizabeth replied. "I've heard stories of the tough places they went with that camera. Not everyone wants you to see what happens to animals behind closed doors."

"I know. She's always getting on me to make better choices. Analyzes my lunch every day and asks me where the ingredients came from. Got me to buy a steer this fall. Said it's my responsibility to be decent to the planet for Benny's sake."

"Admit it," Elizabeth said. "She's getting the job."

"I can't go telling her that yet," Kade said. "In my experience, their heads swell up and they get sloppy. I've got a car show to run."

"I get the feeling she's anything but sloppy," Elizabeth said. He'd levered himself atop the desk, one foot on the ground, the other on the desk chair.

"Raj was a big fan." Kade paused. Elizabeth waited for the subject change, but Kade continued. "I trust his opinion more than most anyone's."

Elizabeth ran a finger down the glossy white wall. A calendar of classic cars hung on a nail near her shoulder. Miss July was an emerald green Studebaker. "Leia wouldn't be half the trained dog she is without Raj."

"He would tell me to hire Alma now, before anyone else figured out we had a gem. We need people with a solid work ethic. Half the apprentices spend most of the day on their phones. I found one on a car flipping site."

"Car flipping?"

"Like houses, but you fix up cars and sell them for a hefty profit. Lots of people make bank on that, but I can't have mechanics more focused on their side job than what's going on in the shop. Not to mention a female mechanic is a rarity. Dang. I need to make her an offer. If Raj were here, he'd kick me."

A few drawers in one cabinet stood open. Papers were stacked in a giant pile on the desk. Invoices and financials, the occasional slip of notes. Elizabeth shifted, and a few fluttered to the floor. She bent to retrieve them and put them back in place. "Speaking of Raj, the deputies are gone?"

"Left right before you arrived. Took what they needed. At least I think they did. Downloaded all sorts of footage. Took Raj's tablet, too. Said I'll get it back...eventually."

"Into an evidence bag?" Elizabeth frowned.

"Not a big deal since we're down a few people but still... It's not a good feeling."

"What was on all that video?"

"Not a whole lot. From what I can tell, they wanted to see who Raj interacted with. Customers and such. What those interactions were like."

"Interesting. He seemed like a standup mechanic."

"One of the best. Most of the videos were him doing regular mechanic things. Changing out transmissions. Rehabilitating air conditioners. Upholstery work. They asked me about any tips or kickbacks, and I didn't have anything to say. Occasionally, people hand us extra cash for good work. There is no way for me to have them claim it on our receipts, so I don't say anything." Kade shrugged.

"Expecting the IRS to beat down your door?"

"That'll be the day. I need to get a bookkeeper back in here, at least part time." He looked at the stacks of paper, the files removed and re-stacked in the investigation. "There was one thing they found in the footage."

"Something on video?"

"Yeah." Kade paused, as though deciding whether to tell her. "Raj pushed an envelope toward a client across the counter."

"An envelope?" Elizabeth couldn't find the sensational in office supplies. "They got excited about an envelope."

"That's the problem," Kade said. "Or the beginning of the problem. I don't have any envelopes that match the one they saw. They searched every inch of this place, despite me telling them that they wouldn't find any. Guess it's not part of their job to take someone's word."

"What was in the envelope?"

"That's the second part of the problem. I have no idea. On my laptop screen, the footage is pretty small, but it looks normal. A standard large brown envelope." Kade reached in the sack and removed another pastry. He peeled off a layer from the outside of the cinnamon roll.

"Manila," Elizabeth said.

"Huh?"

"The color of those envelopes."

"Ah. Well, we do have envelopes, but not the large type. We've got the kind for keys. Small ones. Also the type that comes with the cut out. You know, for a client's address to show through. But that's it."

Elizabeth turned back to the bays as she considered the situation. "He gave it to a customer? Maybe it came out of their car."

Kade tilted his head, considering. "Possible, but that's not what we typically do."

"What do you do?"

Before he could answer, Alma knocked on the window glass, then opened the door. "Polishing done. You could eat off that undercarriage it's so shiny. Next up?"

"Guess I'd better send you off for a real lunch. Break time."

"You don't have to tell me twice.." Alma reached for her bag on a hook. Clipped to the strap was a silver disco ball keychain that sparkled under the fluorescent lights in the office. The Tardis was all about style.

"Actually," Kade said, standing up. "Before you go—a quick quiz for the rookie. What would you do if you found something in a vehicle that you thought might belong to the owner?"

"I assume you mean something other than candy wrappers, water bottles, and sunglasses?" Kade nodded, and Alma continued. "Tell you. If you weren't there, I'd tell Raj. When he was here. Have y'all lock it up in the safe until the person comes to get it. At least that's what Raj said I should do. Next question?"

"You aced the test, proving once again you know your stuff."

Alma smiled and, with a salute, left the shop.

Elizabeth eyed the heavy metal container under the desk. The dial on the front was numbered from zero to one hundred. "Seems secure."

"She's right. If I wasn't here, Raj would lock it up and tell me when I got back. We log the stuff on here." He poked at a clipboard atop the safe. "That way, we know when we found it, who picked it up and when. We only release items to the owner of the car. I can't tell you how many times I leave a voicemail only to have the boyfriend or girlfriend show up and demand whatever it is. How am I supposed to know whether they would give it back or pawn it? A strict policy keeps us out of trouble. Most days, the person is back within an hour, not trusting us to keep a close eye on their stuff."

"Any reason he wouldn't have told you about it this time?"

Doubt creased the lines at Kade's temples. His gaze fell on the list. Kade chewed on the inside of his lip. "Maybe if he thought I wouldn't believe him."

28

Kade pulled up the video on the laptop in his office. Elizabeth stood behind his shoulder. She watched with growing unease as Raj came into the frame behind the short counter. He'd set an invoice on top of a padded manila envelope. He put both hands on top of the stack while he engaged in what looked like casual banter with a customer.

Raj had a casual posture, shoulders relaxed, the picture of ease. The other man, an older man, had a fresh tan and a tropical shirt. They appeared to exchange a few pleasantries, a casual back and forth.

At the end of the conversation, Raj slid the stack toward the man. The man nodded, slid the stack off the counter and into his hands. He flashed a last smile, then exited the shop.

"What do you think that's all about?" Elizabeth asked, her eyes still fixed on the screen.

Kade hit replay and the video looped. They watched the brief exchange again. "I'm not sure," Kade admitted. He tilted back in his office chair and crossed his arms. "But it's not typical."

Elizabeth furrowed her brow. "Could it be something else? Something not related to mechanics."

"What do you mean?"

"I'm thinking about the teacher's lounge. We exchange books, knitting patterns, extra jars of pickles. You know, things like recipes for the best brownies or toddler clothes we aren't using anymore. Maybe Raj and this guy have something else in common."

"It's possible," said Kade. "But Raj wasn't someone to mix business with pleasure. Believe it or not, he kind of kept to himself most of the time. Had an apartment in town. Not much else going on."

"Huh. What did he like to do in his free time?"

Kade pulled a photograph down from the wall and held it out to Elizabeth. "He played club soccer in the summers. And I think he did some of that online gaming. You know the one where you're like a warrior or an elf or something."

Elizabeth searched the image of Raj for explanation, a clue. He sported a polo shirt and whistle, circled up in a group with a dozen kids in uniform. "I've heard of it."

"But that's about it. Not much that would explain what's in the envelope," Kade said.

Elizabeth nodded and handed the frame back to Kade. "Who is that guy in the video? Know him?"

Kade hesitated. "I do. Guy Henderson. One of our best customers. Deals in vintage cars." He opened the office door and headed for the farthest bay.

"A car salesman?" Elizabeth called to his back. She followed him across the shop.

"Not quite. It's not his day job. He's a tech guy. Sold some big app and is still involved to some degree. Dealing with vintage cars is a lucrative hobby. A passion project. Thing is, I'm not sure how above board everything is." Kade operated the switches on the automatic doors, one at a time.

Elizabeth's eyes widened in surprise. "What do you mean? Are you into something you shouldn't be?

"It's not that. Everything Henderson does with us is on paper—accounted for." Kade moved closer and lowered his voice. "Let's just say there are rumors. About his businesses."

Elizabeth's stomach twisted at the thought. "You mean it's not like he posts a for sale sign on the corner and the deal is done in a driveway."

"I don't have any solid proof. It's a solid hunch, though. He ships a lot of them overseas, too."

Elizabeth prided herself on honesty. The idea of shady business associations made her queasy. "So, what do we do now?"

Kade shrugged. "I'm not sure. The officers have this clip. I don't know if they'll let me know what they find—if anything—but they are aware of it."

"When did this happen?" Elizabeth's mind was working through the details. She couldn't shake the need to know what was in that envelope.

"About a month ago. The client hasn't been in since."

Elizabeth trailed a hand along a workbench. "I mean, I *try* not to be here all the time but my car decides otherwise."

"But see, that's the other thing that's a little bit odd. Normally, he would send a couple employees to pick up cars. He has staff who come through, drop off and pick up the cars. I rarely see him outside the car club meetings."

"Too big a deal to do the little things?" Elizabeth watched Kade pick up a few scraps of paper, a stray tool, and right the slight disorder of the work spaces.

"He's one of the board members of the club and a founder of the show. I need to tread with caution."

Elizabeth nodded. "I get it. You can't afford to have your reputation tarnished with shady deals. At the same time, you can't afford to not work with him."

"When you put it like that..." He peeked out a door to the back lot, then locked it closed. "Not everyone in the club is his fan. But he's got a lot of money and influence, so they can't exactly kick him off without reason."

Elizabeth's mind raced as she thought through the details. "So, he and Raj could have been involved in something shady. Or he tried to involve Raj. Or..." Elizabeth shrugged. "Maybe it was some forgotten lingerie from the back seat."

"Raj would have told me about that," Kade said. He was quiet, chin in his hand. "I can look back through the files. Can't say I'll find anything. Raj followed rules. Still."

Elizabeth bit her lip, thinking. "It's a start. And the officers might ask you for that anyway. Even if you turn up nothing, you're prepared for the paperwork."

"But what if I turn up more than nothing?"

29

"Was there ever a reason not to trust Raj?"

"Never gave me a reason not to. Best employee I've ever had." Kade's words trailed off. He rested his chin in his hand.

"Sounds like there's a 'but' in there," Elizabeth said.

Kade sighed. "The garage is my business. I order everything from the gloves people use to every nut and bolt. We don't have anything close to a manila envelope. I can't shake the idea that Raj didn't want me to know about it."

"Any word on how he's doing?"

Kade shook his head and studied the mug in his hands. "Not great is all I know."

Elizabeth sat across from Kade at Beans, a glass of cold brew in her hand. Kade had agreed to meet her there after he closed up shop. Gary had let them in, the last customers of the day, while he cleaned up. They'd commandeered a booth in the back corner. She debated pressing for more details but his crestfallen face changed her mind.

"I've looked into him," Elizabeth said, her eyes fixed on Kade. She slid a pad of notes toward his elbow. "Guy Henderson."

Kade looked from the notes back up to Elizabeth. "That was fast. You sound like a professional."

"I did an internet search, same as anyone." Kade lifted an eyebrow in interest, and Elizabeth continued. "I checked your guest list, too. No surprise, but Guy wasn't at your party, and none of his employees were there either."

"I could have told you that. I sent an invitation, but it came back as a no. He had some out-of-town event."

"I may have been there, but I didn't know half the people in that barn." Elizabeth took a sip of coffee. "I also checked the news stories, and he's in there. Not just for his tech business. He's trying to snap up property."

"Where? Wouldn't surprise me if he had places all over."

"Two spots in Colorado and one here, in Sweetwater County. Apparently, he'd make an offer and then back out at the last minute. The owners sued him for breach of contract. All suits were dismissed, though. No further comment from anyone."

Kade's face darkened. "I'd say it surprises me, but it doesn't. That *Gone with the Wind* stuff about land being one of the best ways to invest isn't far off. He's the type to own a handful of houses."

"I also looked into his alibi the night of the murder. It checks out. He presented at the San Francisco Automotive Expo. It's some industry who's-who kind of night. Cameras on him everywhere."

Kade tilted his chin, listening. "So, he didn't do it. Could be that the envelope is meaningless."

Elizabeth nodded. "Yeah, it seems that way."

Kade sat back in the booth. He picked at a nick in the gray vinyl covering, deep in thought. "I'd be curious to learn the topic that night. What does a guy like that have to say?"

"I don't know much of the tech lingo, but it involves drones," she said.

"An expensive hobby."

"I also checked out his former company. The one he sold. He's still listed as a member of the Board but a non-voting one."

Kade held his cup in both hands. He turned it side to side between his fingers to examine the Beans logo. "So, what you're saying is that he's there in name only."

Elizabeth shrugged. "Maybe. Might have been part of the agreement when he sold his shares. That's not uncommon."

"Is there anything you can't sleuth out? Color me impressed."

"Ten minutes of research can go a long way."

Kade tipped the rest of his cup down his throat and swallowed. "I should get going. I'm drained. Today rocked me. Alma is good but still a greenhorn. I've got to get there even earlier tomorrow."

He stood as though to leave, and Elizabeth laid her hand on his arm. Kade looked down at her hand and then into her eyes.

"One last thing. I found this picture." Elizabeth slid her phone over to Kade. She'd combed the social media from the event to find the picture of a handful of people, glitzy attire, and bottomless martini glasses.

Kade picked up the phone and stared at the screen. "Yeah, that's him." The image showed the same older man with slicked salt and pepper hair. This time in a suit and tie. "And...some attendees at the expo?"

"Yeah, I didn't recognize them. Then again, I'm not from here."

"There's something here..." Kade tapped the person standing next to Guy. His face was turned away from the camera, bright lights blurring the image. The group, including Guy, gathered with drinks around a cocktail table. "I'm not sure why, but he's familiar."

Elizabeth pursed her lips and considered the image. "It's proof Guy was where he said he was."

"Before I go," Kade said, "let me see that guest list one more time."

30

Jo called to Elizabeth from the couch. "Get in here, get in here. It's on!"

"...stabbed with an everyday garden fork..." The volume on the television could shake the house. Jo perched on the edge of the couch, her eyes riveted to the screen. The blue light from the giant screen cast eerie shadows on the wall.

Elizabeth had driven the miles from town in a haze. Facts and thoughts swam in her head like bubbles. Each time she reached for one, it popped and disappeared. Rather than head down Casey's driveway, she took a different turn off the long dirt road. She wasn't ready to be home yet.

In the Wolfs' entryway, Elizabeth dropped her purse on the door mat. She shut the front door behind her and scooted into the living room. Jo had her knees up, the remote in one hand. Elizabeth joined her.

"What are we watching?"

"Shhh." Jo noticed her guest. "Oh, Liz, hey. Thought you were Clint."

On the screen was the Billings news. The reporter, kitted out in a jacket with the station's emblem on the chest, clutched a microphone into which he spoke with authority. With a wide stance and a confident air, he commanded the screen space.

"...asked that if you have any leads to call the Johnson County Sheriff's tip line. I'm Preston Powers, and this is News on Your Side."

Jo turned off the television with a press of a button and tossed the remote onto the coffee table. "You missed most of it. Must have been a slow day in the big city for them to send someone all the way down here."

"What exactly did I miss?"

"Press conference. Well, what little they had of one. They have a person of interest in the case and are pursuing all leads. Classic lines. First they showed a picture of Raj. You know, the one from the bike race. Poor guy. Then they showed the courthouse and then that guy"—she pointed at the ghost of Preston's image—"was standing on Kade's road, near his house."

"Kade's going to love that," Elizabeth said, and grimaced.

"It's just a hunch, but Kade Michaels doesn't seem like the type who looks for an audience."

"Maybe no one will recognize that road. At least no one who matters." Elizabeth picked up one of Jo's couch pillows. One side was quilted, each block a star with smaller stars inside. Blue and white triangles were sewn in radiating patterns. The back had initials embroidered in one corner. "We had coffee this afternoon."

Jo tented an eyebrow. "And?"

"They collected some of his video footage from the shop. Security cameras. Went through the garage, checked Raj's locker."

"Find anything?"

"Some footage of Raj with a customer, and there are questions about interactions. Nothing obvious though."

"The newscast said there were inquiries into the victim's business dealings."

"News travels fast, then. The thing is, I can't picture Raj as someone who would get involved in anything sketchy."

Jo got to her feet. "Can I get you something? At this point, I'm going to have a liquid dinner, waiting for my husband to grace me with his presence. I've made two grocery lists and a spreadsheet for our campsite for when that man finally takes a vacation next month."

"I'm good." When Jo disappeared into the kitchen, Elizabeth let her gaze settle on the room. A mantle decked in framed pictures, a shawl draped over the back of the chair. She missed Rhett and Casey. Wanted to get back to them. "I should get home soon, actually."

Jo returned with a glass of water she pressed into Elizabeth's hands. "Get hydrated, then go. My dermatologist said I'm not doing myself any favors if I don't drink half my weight in water. I've got an app now and everything."

"Do you?" Elizabeth eyed the glass and then took a long drink. "Guessing I'd better get on board. It's a short drive if I need a pit stop. Where's yours?"

"Downed it before the show, so I could move on to other selections." Jo wrapped her fingers around the stem of her glass and circled it in the air. Burgundy wine swirled around the glass. When Jo stilled her hand, the liquid dripped in streaks down the inside surface. "You were there. What do you think?"

Elizabeth frowned. "What do you mean?"

"You knew Raj some. Do you have any reason to think he was involved in anything questionable?"

"No way was he involved. Jeez, Jo. He was stabbed in Kade's front yard. In the back. It wasn't a shoot-out at the O.K. Corral."

"He does have a past," Jo said, then drained her glass. "Don't know if Kade told you that."

Elizabeth shook her head. "Kade mentioned something, but so what? I've got a past, too. Doesn't mean I can't do better, be better than I was. Are we always shackled to our past selves?"

"A lot of that is a choice..."

"What is with all the cloaked answers today?"

"Must be in the water. That's what my mama would say," Jo said. She followed Elizabeth to the front door. "Look, you know I believe in fresh starts more than most. Couldn't keep my head upright in this community if I didn't. But time has taught me that sometimes, when you least expect it, the past has a way of coming back to bite you in the tush."

31

The chain of the swing squeaked as its rider stretched his toddler feet toward the sky. Black vinyl formed the bucket in which he sat, more secure than the banana-style for older kids. His small hands gripped the chains as his head tilted back. A breeze whispered through his hair as he looked up at the clouds.

"Thank you for giving me another shot."

"As long as you don't think it's standard practice," Elizabeth said. "The last thing I want is people thinking they can bail on me whenever they like without consequences. That'd wreak havoc on my parent-teacher conferences."

"Scouts' honor," Kade said, making a sign with one hand. With the other, he held the end of a teeter totter. Across the platform sat Benny. Kade levered the seesaw to lift and lower his nephew.

Benny paid little attention to the rhythmic change in altitude. He had a travel size pair of binoculars slung around his neck. Each time a bird flew by, he brought the lenses to his face.

"American crow." A few minutes later, he said, "Red tail hawk." Then, a triumphant, "Western Meadowlark, state bird of Wyoming and five other states!"

Kade had sent Elizabeth a text to ask if there was a chance to meet at the park and make up for last time. He'd said Alma could handle the rest of the day's business. He was due an afternoon off.

Elizabeth waited a full fifteen minutes before replying, then chided herself. *Don't be ridiculous*, she thought, and picked up the phone to text. It was time to be up front and honest. After all, she'd promised Jo she'd be direct. Over text, they hatched a plan, and now here they were.

Two adults, two kids, and two dogs. At a park together. *Like a family.*

Sunlight glinted off the expansive equipment. A gaggle of kids clambered over the climbing structure, zipping up and down the slides. Shouts and giggles accompanied their play. A teenage-couple held hands from adjacent swings, toes trailing in the bark chips.

Elizabeth scanned the field of the dog enclosure for Leia and Brutus. The pair sniffed at the base of an old cottonwood. Brutus lifted his leg. The dogs were happy to be off-leash with no agenda other than sleuthing out which dogs had been there first. Elizabeth figured they were all right on their own, at least until another dog arrived. The two were a bonded pair, well-used to a pack of other dogs around, and Leia was a trained therapy dog. Still, Elizabeth didn't want to be one of those owners who abandoned their pup.

They'd brought the dogs for exercise. For the first twenty minutes, Kade played fetch within the confines of the chain link-fenced area. Every other throw resulted in a wrestling match. The dogs wanted more, but the kids needed a change of scenery.

Summer afternoon heat radiated off the cement and play structures. A sheen of sweat covered Elizabeth's brow. She'd had the time to toss together her favorite bake sale cookies and mix a batch of lavender lemonade. Both were recipes she planned to serve at the opening at the art gallery. *Practice makes perfect.*

Their easy banter dissolved into a moment of silence that settled in the grass like a picnic blanket. Elizabeth snuck a glance at Kade. He stared off into the distance, a crease between his brows.

"A penny for your thoughts?"

"Hmm? Oh. Nothing much. Off in space."

Elizabeth caught and launched Rhett in arcs through the air. Between pushes, she snuck a peek at Kade. "You said Alma had everything under control. She must be working out."

The teenagers moved off, and Benny replaced one of them in a swing. Kade stepped behind his nephew to push. "She really is. We had a quiet enough afternoon, and she was ready. She was going to put the Tardis on a lift, give that old boat some time." Kade frowned and pulled his phone from the shirt pocket at his chest. It vibrated in audible protest. "Sorry, just a sec."

He turned from the swing set after giving Benny a big push. Elizabeth took over and alternated between the two swings. She overheard snippets of Kade's conversation.

"What?...You're kidding...No, he didn't. Uh huh...But that's ridiculous...Of course...I'm at the park. Yep, I'll be here."

"Everything okay?"

Kade shook his head, a slight, perceptible shift of disbelief. "I pulled files, like you suggested. My bookkeeper went through them. Apparently, she found something."

32

The balsa wood airplane sailed across the sidewalk and plopped into a boxwood bush. Rhett clapped and bounced at the result of Benny's launch. Elizabeth plucked the aircraft from its landing spot and gave it back to the six-year-old. Benny sent it sailing through the air again. This time, he took off after it and chased its flight plan. He reached up to catch it, mid-air.

Kade remained silent for the ten minutes between the call and the arrival of a silver sedan into the parking lot. Elizabeth's mouth fell open when Venus—Becky—stepped out of the car. The woman made a beeline for Kade. Elizabeth talked herself out of the petty glare she longed to deliver.

Kade met her before she made it all the way to the playground. Both dogs had ears up, trained on the interloper. Brutus stretched and stood, an elongation of his spine, ready to intervene.

"It's okay, you two," Elizabeth said, as though they understood her. The dogs were leashed to a picnic table. When Elizabeth didn't react to the new person, Leia returned her chin to her paws. Elizabeth continued to keep one eye on the boys and one on Kade and his newest employee.

Becky pressed a folder of papers into Kade's hands. He flipped through them, eyes widening with each new document. As Elizabeth watched, he closed the folder and shook his head. Without another word to Becky, he started their way. Elizabeth turned her attention back to the boys as though she hadn't been watching.

"I have to make a call," he said when he reached them. "Would you mind watching them for a minute?"

"Sure," she said, but he'd already walked away from them.

Several paces away, Kade pressed the phone to his ear. As his voice rose, so did his gestures, unseen by the person at the other end of the line. Elizabeth couldn't tell what he was saying but knew his words weren't something he wanted her, the boys, or anyone else, to hear.

"This is a lot for him," said a voice at Elizabeth's side. Becky stood next to her, eyes on Kade. "He doesn't need you adding to it."

"Excuse me?"

Becky gave Elizabeth a tight smile. "I know your type. Single mom, extra baggage—at this age. You're looking for a good guy. Someone who isn't too complicated. Strong, yet sensitive. Outdoorsy. You try to act the part of a confident, independent woman, but on the inside, you're a mess of self-doubt and regret. Desperation written all over your face. Kade doesn't need that in his life."

Before Elizabeth could splutter out a response, Becky took off after Kade. Elizabeth started to follow but stopped when she saw Kade return the paperwork to his bookkeeper. Becky reached out to touch his arm, then headed back to her car. Elizabeth could see the woman's glare through the windshield as she started the engine.

"I'm sorry," Kade said on approach. He held out his hands as though about to explain, then let them drop at his sides.

"What happened?"

"Those papers. They're work orders for a single client."

"Yeah?"

Kade rubbed at the back of his neck. "The dates check out. Last month, Raj started billing that company for the work until sometime after they were picked up."

Elizabeth turned that over in her mind. "You mean they didn't pay when they picked them up—but later?"

"Something like that. I'm having Becky run through everything again. Some may have sat on our lot until they sold, but I need dates. We can check VINs."

"Am I wrong to assume people are supposed to pony up when they collect their car?"

"Garage policy says we collect when you collect. And Raj only did this for that client. Only this client. And it's a recent thing."

"Let me guess, it's Mr. Video."

The boys squatted in the grass to examine an ant hill. Benny pointed and described his observations as a wide-eyed Rhett looked on.

Kade pressed his palms together to rest his chin on his steepled fingertips. "I've got to hand this over to the deputies, don't I?"

33

Enid's mass of curls twisted like undulating snakes atop her head. The cafe owner flipped switches and pulled handles behind the shiny espresso machine. Enid adored Old Betsy. The machine was a special order from Europe. She'd bestowed the name upon the device when it arrived. She and her barista, Gary, polished the chrome with practiced regularity. Their attention wasn't unlike that of a car owner, proud to show off gleaming surfaces to every admirer.

Today, however, Enid swore under her breath. She blamed Betsy for scalding the milk. "Darn finicky machine. A bit like a cat, this one. Go with the flow and she'll do right by you, but the minute you need something specific, it's all protest." Enid poured the ruined milk into the little sink behind the bar. She set the carafe in the dish bin and grabbed for a new pitcher. "I blame Gary. The man had the audacity to take a day off and leave me here to flounder."

"No stress on my part, please," Elizabeth said. "I'll take an Americano with a splash of cream."

"You're a saint." Enid poured the espresso into the mug. She added a touch of hot water followed by a splash of cream from a glass bottle. "Is that the right shade for you?"

Elizabeth peered at the swirling liquid. White and brown intermingled. "Looks perfect. Smells even better. I started drinking these this fall. It's the only thing my coworker knows how to make, so she brews them up for everyone. I've learned to like them."

"Now that's the spirit."

"Eh, we can tell when she's fighting with her boyfriend. She'll over-extract the espresso in that dinky machine, and the brew gets bitter. I keep a bottle of hazelnut syrup in my desk for those days. Don't tell her."

"Your secret is safe with me." Enid began to clean the machine in preparation for the next customer.

Elizabeth dug in her pocket for her wallet. She'd left the house with few belongings, intending to run a few quick errands. "What do I owe you?"

"It's on the house—as long as you fill me in on Kade. Jo is tight-lipped. Said she wouldn't break the code of trust between you two. She likes to lord secrets over me."

"Would you do the same?"

"You know it. Now spill. *Please.* I could use a little vicarious romance in my life." Enid slid a raspberry macaron Elizabeth's way and selected one for herself.

The chef waited, attentive in her apron, flour streaked across one shirt sleeve. Elizabeth had left the house in jogger leggings and a brewery shirt. In contrast to Enid's mane, Elizabeth had wound her hair into a dancer's bun atop her forehead.

Elizabeth told Enid about the afternoon at the park. The sight of the boys and dogs playing together. The moment when it all felt right. "But I'm scared. What if I mess it all up? I'm not known to manage these situations well." Elizabeth stared into her cup as though it held fortune-telling tea leaves instead of coffee.

"Is that true, or is that your excuse to avoid taking a risk?" Enid peered over the rim of her own mug at Elizabeth.

Elizabeth sucked in her cheeks. "Both?"

The bell over the shop door jingled, and Enid straightened, prepared to return to her role as barista. "We talk ourselves out of next best steps all the time in the name of caution. Being afraid is easy. It's bravery that takes work."

"Elizabeth is one of the bravest women I've ever met," Alma said. She'd joined the duo at the counter. The apprentice mechanic wore her coveralls, hair in two braids over her shoulders. She pried off the lid to her to-go cup and passed it to Enid. "I watched her chase a murderer up a mountainside on a snowmobile and live to tell the tale."

"May I never have to do that again," Elizabeth said, as a smile tugged at the corner of her lips. "You were no weakling that day, either. I've seen you go toe-to-toe with a challenger like it was nothing."

Enid finished Alma's regular order and returned the cup. She added a macaron on a napkin. Alma fished a wad of bills from her hip bag for Enid.

"Cheers to brave women," Enid said, and held her own beverage high in the air.

Alma raised her travel mug and clinked it against Elizabeth's cup before taking a sip. "What is it that requires a big dose of courage?"

Elizabeth said, "Nothing, really," at the same time Enid said, "She *likes* someone."

"Ooh, you do? Who?" Alma's eyebrows rose in curiosity as she shifted her attention between the two women. Enid's grin stretched from ear to ear as she winked at Alma.

Elizabeth hesitated long enough for Enid to mouth, "Kade."

Alma leaned in, eyes sparkling with excitement. "That's awesome! You two would make a great couple."

Elizabeth blushed, a flutter in her stomach. "Thanks. I mean, there's nothing...official. It's a...crush at this point. And I'm nervous. I've got a kid to think about. So does Kade. And a business."

"And everything that happened to Raj," Enid added.

Alma nodded. "I get it. That's a lot. But you have nothing to worry about. Be yourself. Listen to your gut and everything will be fine."

Elizabeth smiled at Alma's reassurance. She was grateful for words of wisdom from someone her junior. "Thanks, Alma. That means a lot. And please, not a word about this conversation to Kade. It's all so new."

Alma looked down at her own phone, flicked her thumb across the screen a few times, then looked up with a grin. "Speaking of nerves, I'm a bit of a wreck about the upcoming car show."

A stream of afternoon shoppers interested in a pick-me-up entered the little cafe. They crowded the counter. Many asked for menus to select from an extensive cookie selection. Elizabeth nudged her chin toward the tables, then picked up her cup and saucer and headed over to claim one. Alma followed.

Elizabeth could see Enid's mane bob behind the machine as she churned out drinks. "What's going on?"

Alma pressed her palms to the tabletop. "I decided to enter the Tardis. I'm a little late, but I got notice that they found a spot for me. This is my first show, but I've been working on restoration for months. I want to show off my work, make some connections, get some feedback," Alma said, a gleam in her eye.

Elizabeth appraised the pride in her seatmate. The woman worked hard, whether from behind a camera or underneath a classic car. "I'm sure it will be a showstopper."

Alma beamed. "I hope so. I've got a few days to get it ready. Well, as ready as I can. We are absolute bonkers at the garage. Appointments are double-booked for show prep and with no Raj..."

"That's a lot of pressure," Elizabeth said. Kade had apologized for needing to leave the other afternoon by securing a real date. Just the two of them. *Yipes.* "What do you know about Kade's new bookkeeper?"

Alma lifted one shoulder in a half shrug. "Becky? Not much. Used to be big in horses. Rich husband died and she has to work to pay the bills. Has a taste for expensive shoes. Why?"

"I was curious. Kade said she was a rehire."

Alma twisted the cap of her travel mug and nodded. "Used to work there a long time ago. He hired her to help us keep up with the paperwork volume around the show. Temporary job."

Elizabeth breathed a sigh of relief. *Is it wrong to be glad Becky won't be around for long?* "Makes sense."

"She's his neighbor," she said, off-hand. "Well, as much as people can be neighbors when they have a hundred acres. Seems happy to help out. And she is good at it. Streamlined our flow. Set up digital billing."

"I bet that helped." Elizabeth frowned. She didn't like to think of Kade relying on this woman.

"Maybe..." Alma wiped up leftover crumbs from the tiny cafe tabletop with an abandoned napkin. She folded the paper into quarters to contain the bits. "Raj sure didn't like her."

Elizabeth felt a chill run down her spine. "Oh?"

"Yeah. Couldn't put my finger on why. He had this irritated look whenever she was around. Like her presence crawled across his skin. Watched her every chance he got."

"Maybe they knew each other from someplace else?" Elizabeth considered Alma's words. She thought of the Raj she'd known at work.

Bubbly. Energetic. Cheerful and kind to all. If someone gave him the reaction Alma described, there had to be a reason. "Any idea why she left the job in the first place?"

Alma palmed the napkin and scanned the room for the nearest trash can. "Boss didn't say much to any of us. She showed up a few weeks ago and that was that. He's been so focused on the apprentice program, then the show."

"The life of a small business owner," Elizabeth said. A twitch of guilt tugged at her mind. Would it have been easier on Kade to schedule their date after the show? They'd waited months to get together, one more week wouldn't hurt. Elizabeth could hear Jo's voice in her head. *Sounds like an excuse to chicken out, Elizabeth Blau.* Further, she needed to be cautious with Becky. Rude or not, the woman helped Kade. It was hard to resent someone who made good things possible for people you cared about. "I'm sure he appreciates the help."

Alma shook her head. "Some days it's like he hardly sees anyone. He's too focused on a task list. But I've been keeping an eye on her. She's been staying late at work, going through files and papers. I don't know what she's up to, but it's more than overtime."

34

Elizabeth rummaged through her meager wardrobe. She rejected one pair of jeans as too casual and tossed them to the floor. On top, she tossed the single dress she owned. Wearing what she wore to her last first date's funeral was not the look she was after. She draped her favorite capris over the bedspread. Above them, she fanned a rainbow of blouse options and turned to her audience. "What do you think? Tan with white stripes or navy with tan stripes?"

"What about that frilly top you wore to Easter? The one with the trees?"

"Conifers," Elizabeth said. "Won't work. I love the pattern, but those nylon blends make me itch something fierce. I can't have Kade thinking I have some sort of uncontrollable skin disease."

Jo smirked. "Especially if you plan to show him any of that skin."

Elizabeth threw a wadded up sweater at Jo. Jo caught the knit top and shook it out. "This one isn't too bad."

"If it was about twenty degrees cooler. I'm already sweating like a pig, and I'm not even on the date. The last thing I need is to crank up the heat with my wardrobe."

Jo eyed her friend, then tossed the sweater onto the bed. "Okay, how about navy with tan? That way, if you spill something, it won't stand out."

"Thanks for your faith in my basic manners." Elizabeth rolled her eyes.

Jo had agreed to come over and supervise date preparation. She would serve double duty as babysitter when it was time for Elizabeth to leave.

Elizabeth slipped into the suggested shirt, twisted this way and that. Again, she approached the mirror, frowned, and viewed herself from the back side.

Jo watched from the bed and suppressed a grin. "You're terrified, aren't you?"

Elizabeth huffed at her reflection. She tugged first at one corner of the shirt, then the other. She tucked the front into her pants, examined herself, then tucked in the rest. "It's not every day I go on a date." After another mirror check, she untucked the shirt and swapped it out for another. This one was floral, a burgundy covered with tiny roses.

Jo raised an eyebrow. "I thought you and Kade were already friends, right? Think of it as a night out with a friend, that's all."

"We are, but this feels different. It is different. Sure, we're friends now, but I could send that downhill real fast."

Jo chuckled. "Relax, Liz. Kade likes you. You don't need to impress him."

"That may be, but he's taking time off from a huge workload to spend time with me," Elizabeth said to the mirror. She smoothed the navy and tan-striped top back over her head. I don't want him to end up regretting it when he's up to his ears in a backlog of cars. Guilt is eating me up."

"Maybe consider feeling special instead. Everyone needs a break from time to time. He's choosing to spend this one with you. He's even bringing the food."

Elizabeth pawed through her scant jewelry box. She sought earrings that fell between schoolteacher studs and giant hoops she'd kept from college. Why were Jo's words hard to hear? *Because you don't think you deserve that kind of attention,* Elizabeth thought. Her own doubts were a gut punch to her conscience. "Eighty-three percent of women are attracted to men who can cook."

"Maybe he's trying to ensnare you the old-fashioned way. If he serves nothing but oysters and dark chocolate, you have my permission to head for the hills."

Elizabeth selected a set of pearl drop earrings that belonged to her mother. She slipped them into her ears and attached the backs. "Heard anything in Raj's case?"

"Clint hasn't heard much. Johnson County is tight-lipped. Kade say anything?" Jo reached for a laundry basket and began to pair up the socks.

Elizabeth shook her head. "Nothing. He's been so focused on the show and the dwindling ranks of his employees."

Jo started in on Rhett's shirts. She folded each into a tight square. "I don't know about you, but I'm still not sleeping well."

"My dreams have been far from great." Elizabeth had tossed and turned so much her sheets were twisted each morning. She'd had the same dream several nights in a row. There she was, walking with Kade down a winding path through a dark wood. In the distance, they'd see a gleaming object. Something bright through the trees. As they neared the object, the view would become clearer, their surroundings less hazy. Before she could identify the object, she'd wake up in a cold sweat.

"Could be the heat," Jo said.

"Could be." Elizabeth tried to stuff down the idea that Raj was involved in anything shady. She'd yet to tell Jo about the discrepancies

Becky found in the books. It wasn't her secret to tell. Even if there was something off, Raj didn't deserve what happened. The visual of his body on the path again flooded her thoughts. Elizabeth squeezed her eyes shut.

Jo put both hands on Elizabeth's shoulders. "Liz. It will be okay. I'm going to take Rhett. We'll have a proper slumber party at which we will watch cartoons, stuff our faces with brownies, and fall asleep by eight. Stay out as long as you like. You and Kade are good people. You both deserve a decent night out together. Now go and have one before anything else happens."

35

It will be okay. Elizabeth repeated the words to herself as she and Kade arrived at the park for the concert.

The sun pitched itself over the horizon. Stars popped into place behind, scattered sequins in the night. Elizabeth remembered Becky's costume, the way she shimmied in the bodysuit. Perhaps she was at the garage right now, researching Raj's past all while knowing her boss was on a date with Elizabeth. A pinch of glee nipped at Elizabeth's conscience.

When they reached the grassy area, they picked their way across the space. Elizabeth pushed Kade's employee from her mind and turned her attention back to her date. Families and couples were scattered across the lawn, awaiting the show. Many sprawled on blankets dotted with small coolers. Each staked out a defined territory for the evening. Children chased tight circles around the adults, whooping and hollering into the night air. A few dogs watched from the ends of leashes. The faint hum of insects and the trickle of Big Goose Creek welcomed them to Kendrick Park.

As they wove through the crowd to find a spot, Elizabeth couldn't help but scan the faces of the people around her. She couldn't shake the feeling that whoever had attacked Raj could be in the crowd. That night again, the news had flashed a call for any information on the case, a photograph of Raj's face plastered on the screen.

In an open spot, Kade unfurled his blanket and set a basket on top. From within, he withdrew a bottle of wine and several containers. He busied himself with the preparations.

While he set up their feast, Elizabeth scoped out the stage. Under a large covering, rows of chairs and music stands arced outward to hold a sizable band. Several musicians took their places early to tune their instruments. The trombone player mimed his upcoming movements, a silent guide playing in his head. The brass slider flashed in the light as the player went through the motions of a song. Something about the curve of his jaw was familiar, down to the Celtic tattoo on the inside of one arm.

Kade set out a charcuterie feast at their feet. Thin slices of salami, a buttery brie, and the tiny pickles that were her brother's favorite. As they ate, Elizabeth glanced at those in their vicinity. Eavesdropped on their conversations. People chatted with those around them. Some about the show, others about their work, the kids. How their mother was holding up. One family passed out popsicles to any kid who passed by. Blue raspberry-colored tongues were all the rage as children danced and skipped about. *Rhett might like to come to this,* she thought. *If it isn't too loud.*

It struck Elizabeth that, to the other concertgoers, she and Kade must look like any other couple. Two people enjoying each other's company. Together.

As the rest of the musicians made their way to the stage, Kade passed her a glass bowl and a fork. Inside was a hearty Greek salad composed of quinoa, cucumbers, chickpeas, red onions, feta, and grilled chicken. Before she could take a bite, he brandished a tiny jar of dressing from the basket. The lid was labeled *lemon tahini* and smelled like a day on the coast of the Aegean Sea. As his final touch, he used a portable pepper grinder to crack fresh grounds over their bowls. Last, he extracted a multitool from his pocket and flicked out the bottle opener. He went to work on the cork and soon, both her stomach and her heart were full and happy. "Thank you," she said. "This is incredible."

"You're welcome," he said. "I'm glad it worked out. I've been looking forward to tonight like you can't imagine."

Crimson spread across her cheeks as blood pounded in her ears. Kade brushed a crumb from her cheek, and Elizabeth turned her face to kiss his thumb.

The shuffling and scraping of chairs on the stage interrupted their moment as the conductor took to the stage with the rest of the musicians.

Elizabeth needed a minute to slow her pulse enough to eat.

The evening was a collection of big band hits. As the park transformed into a magical concert hall under the stars, her wariness dissolved. Gratitude took its place. Elizabeth's mood lifted with every note. When she finished her food, Kade whisked the bowl away and replaced it with his hand. He returned his attention to the music, tapping his foot along with every measure.

Elizabeth looked down at their hands entwined. She wished to hold on to this moment, to savor the sweetness of a perfect summer evening.

After a rousing round of applause, the band director stepped to the microphone. "For our second half of tonight's program, we are bringing on more of the pops side of our pops orchestra. We'll be joined by the brass section for a jazzy end to the evening. Don't go far, and we'll see you back here in fifteen minutes."

At intermission, Kade suggested getting an ice cream. Elizabeth agreed. She craved something sweet and a chance to stretch her legs.

Hand in hand, they crossed the grass to join the line for cones. When Kade pulled out his phone to flip through some texts, Elizabeth scanned the crowd. Most in line were families, eager to buy a half dozen single scoops for a gaggle of kids whose ice cream would drip down their hands as it melted. Couples shared milkshakes. An elderly woman ordered butter pecan for an extra moment of nostalgia. As Casey said, there was always room for ice cream as it filled in the cracks.

Her gaze landed on a man near the order window. He was familiar in the way that residents of their county began to swim in her mind, the new sea of people in which she'd slowly begun to swim.

She tilted her head to get a better view, but the line shifted. After he received his ice cream, the man turned around to leave. When his eyes found Elizabeth—or was it Kade?—they went wide in panic. She tried to get a closer look, but the man disappeared around the ice cream stand before she could point him out.

Elizabeth racked her brain for his identity. Who was he—and more importantly, why had he run off?

Kade stuffed his phone back in his pocket. "Sorry, it's Alma's first night closing up by herself so that I could be here with you. I was about to ask for your favorite ice cream flavor."

Elizabeth opened her mouth to answer when a scream pierced through the crowd.

36

Shouts and more screams echoed across the lawn.

"Stay here," Kade said. He held one hand out as though to hold her back. "I'll find out what happened."

"That's not my style," Elizabeth said, and took off after him.

Panting, they reached the stage to join a crowd of people gathered at its lip. One woman lay in a nearby lawn chair, limbs askew, while people fanned her. Another woman stood outside the group, shaking her head and crying. The few children nearby were hushed. Subdued and silent, they awaited directions from their parents. Elizabeth couldn't see through the bodies.

"EMT," Kade said, and pushed into the group. "Let me through! Call 911!"

Elizabeth followed in Kade's wake. He had the capable musculature and confidence in this situation as a trained professional. Had he told her this about himself and she'd missed it? She'd been so panicked with Raj, so focused on getting help, she hadn't watched what Kade did.

The crowd parted, their eyes wide and cheeks slack. Elizabeth spotted the source of their upset as they neared the stage.

A trombone lay on its side, shining in the lights. Its bell was dented and dinged, as though it had been thrown, the mouthpiece missing. The slider lay discarded in the grass.

Two people crouched between the rows of chairs and music stands. Kade placed both hands on the edge of the stage to boost himself up and over. Elizabeth remained below. When she saw their focus, her hands flew up to her mouth.

On a pile of music which had fluttered to the ground, knocked loose from a stand, lay someone Elizabeth recognized. The man from earlier at the ice cream stand was supine. The same one who'd reacted to her and Kade joining the line. Now, three people worked above him, each taking turns at CPR compressions. His lips were blue, his eyes vacant, as though staring at the stars winking out in the growing darkness. With growing horror, Elizabeth pictured him wrapped in a sheet, sandals on his feet, and a beer glass to his lips.

Thor.

Kade and the others focused on their task. One counted, one watched their timer while Kade did chest compressions. Elizabeth thought of her brief CPR training at work. Would she be able to remember any of it in a real emergency?

"The fire truck is here!"

"Step back! Move over."

Firemen approached the crowd, and all stepped back to give access. The red engine parked parallel to the grass. An ambulance slid in behind. The crew ran for the stage, mounting the steps with their equipment.

When the professionals reached the huddled group, Kade and the others stepped back. Elizabeth saw Kade's chest heave deep breaths. It was as though he'd been too focused on trying to save a life to breathe for himself.

"He's gone," someone said in her ear. Elizabeth turned to see the conductor, his eyes blinking. He covered his face with his hands and turned away.

Whispers rippled through the crowd as they watched personnel go through the motions with no result. Children were hustled off, shielded from the sight. In twos and threes, much of the crowd disbanded, hope slashed.

A stretcher was brought for the body.

37

Numb, Elizabeth waited for Kade. She'd moved back to their blanket and packed up the few leftovers. She hugged herself, a tight squeeze of little comfort.

Sheriff Wolf huddled with Kade and the other first responders to take down information and ask questions. He consulted with someone over his radio before stepping down from the stage to talk with the crowd.

Clint had once confessed that talking with people was both the most and least favorite part of his job. He loved educating the public to be safe. Adored attending community events. He wanted to help people when they needed someone to be there. At the same time, much of his work was far from easy. Conversations got tricky, emotional. People didn't like to be in the wrong, and no one wanted tragic news. "You get to where you learn it's more about the delivery, rather than the message," he'd said one night at dinner. She watched him now, his words soft and kind to the scared and curious.

"Please go home," he said. "There's nothing more to be done here. Take care of your loved ones. I'm sorry this happened. Let's give folks their privacy at this time. If you've got anything we need to know, I'll be here to listen."

Flashing lights, red and blue, strobed across the grass. People gathered their things and shuffled off to their cars, moods subdued. Released from his talk with the deputy, Kade made his way back to Elizabeth.

"I'm sorry," he said, shaking his head. "Sheriff needed us to detail what we did to help them sort out what happened to him."

"I didn't know you'd been an EMT."

Kade nodded. "Technically I was a Combat Medic Specialist. Army. It's been almost fifteen years since then, but there are some things you don't forget. No matter how hard you try."

Elizabeth was quiet. This was a new side of Kade, an unexpected kernel of his past. Her impulse to spit out a fact about emergency response rates was quelled by her desire to respect his vulnerability. *Keep it together, Liz.*

"This was not what I pictured for tonight. For our date." Kade's shoulders slumped. He held his hands out to the side then let them fall. "Ever start to feel like the world keeps kicking you when you're down?"

Elizabeth put her hand on his arm. "Hey. This was hardly your fault. And before everything happened...well, the first part was wonderful. I'm sorry it was someone you knew..."

Kade looked at her, the corners of his mouth turned down. His eyes were red-rimmed and watery. "You knew Thor?"

"I recognized him from your party."

"We joked that he hadn't had to dress up. That is...was...his real name." Kade wiped a hand down the front of his face, as if doing so would refresh his expression. "What would you think if we called it a night?"

Elizabeth nodded. As they turned to walk back to Kade's blanket, a flash of sparkle caught her eye. "Just a second," she said, a flicker of recognition pulling her back.

At the edge of the stage was a keychain. A silver disco ball glinted in the lights, red and blue.

38

Elizabeth dangled the tiny, mirrored ball from the finger of one hand. With the other, she spun the sphere. It sparkled in the streetlights. *I'll give it back to Alma. It has to be hers, right?* If it wasn't, then what was it doing on the stage?

Kade waited out the other cars that navigated toward the parking lot exit. He was quiet, expressionless. His eyes tracked the brake lights, the turn signals, and little else. A late evening thundershower rolled in, rain smattering the windshield as they waited.

"I...um. You...I don't know what to say," Elizabeth said. She clutched the ball in her hand and turned back to the window. Drops slid down the glass in rivulets. "I'm sorry. I feel like I should say something and not just sit here."

Kade, eyes on the road, reached over to squeeze her hand, a quick gesture. "You don't have to. That was my job. Trying to help. Before. I just...wanted to leave the past in the past. If that makes sense. Doesn't look like I'll get to, though. At least not yet."

Elizabeth tried to picture Kade as a younger man. Uniformed. Responding to emergencies which she could only imagine. His eyes were blank, as though he was far away. She clasped her hands together and put them between her knees to focus her attention. Anxiety bubbled up, causing her to question whether she should say anything at all.

The slice of moon cast a silver glow over the rooftops of downtown Sheridan. Each block spanning outward meant fewer street lamps and more front yards. Drops splatted on sidewalks. Televisions glowed from within living rooms, and bicycles laid abandoned on porches. Evening settled in, like a dog who'd circled twice and settled in for the night.

As they turned onto Crook Street, Elizabeth pressed her thumbs together, thinking. In a few minutes, they'd be back at the garage, and the date would be over. She would tell Kade thank you and...go home? Given the upset in the park, a kiss didn't seem on the horizon. A handshake was too formal, and a hug didn't fit either.

"Only half of first dates end in a kiss," she blurted, then clapped a hand over her mouth.

Kade glanced at her, eyebrows raised. "Not sure if this counts as a date in anyone's book. Let's try it again another time, yeah?" He returned his gaze to the windshield. "Maybe after the show."

"Yes, please. A redo." Kade's Garage came into view, and the immediacy of the moment pressed at her sternum. "Thanks for the ride."

Kade navigated his truck through the beginnings of a puddle and into the parking lot. "'Course. I'll park near you. I'm going to run in and double check that Alma followed my list."

"Jo would love to hear about that. She's always making lists for me. I hate to think what would happen if she ever ran out of paper." Elizabeth emitted a chuckle, then immediately wished it back inside her mouth. *Get a grip,* she told herself. "I've got something to return of Alma's. I'll set it on her tool chest."

But Kade wasn't listening. Instead, he squinted through the truck window at his shop. Elizabeth looked toward the looming structure.

The door to the customer area was ajar. Inside, the shop was dark, motionless.

"What in the world?" Kade pulled his truck in front of the shop and put it in park. "Stay here," he said, for the second time that night.

"Not happening," Elizabeth said. While his unease became her own, she didn't want to be alone in his truck. "I'm coming with you."

Kade kept his headlights trained on the front of the shop. As they approached, their bodies cast eerie shadows on the bay doors. The shop was silent, still.

With the fingers of his left hand, Kade gave the front door a push. It swung open with a whoosh. When no sound or movement followed, he used the flashlight on his phone to peer inside.

The place was ransacked. Tools were scattered on the ground inside the bays. A bucket had been dumped, its gloppy contents spreading over the concrete. Computer wires hung loose, disconnected.

Kade flicked on all the lights, one bank at a time. Once the space was lit, they could see that the office door was wide open. Every surface and the floor were littered with paper. A cup of coffee was spilled across documents, a chair overturned. Every desk drawer was devoid of its contents, and customer keys were strewn around the room.

Elizabeth's mouth dropped open.

39

"I need to call the police," Kade said. "Before I go on a vigilante rampage." He stepped outside to call, boots crushing glass and other manner of debris.

Elizabeth shrank into the corner, unsure how to support, afraid she'd say the wrong thing. The damage was devastating. When a few papers fluttered to the floor, she bolted outside behind him, startled.

Out front, Kade hung up the phone. While they waited for the police to arrive, they stood in the cool night air, silent. She couldn't help the situation, but leaving didn't seem right.

"Go home," he said, staring off into the night. "I don't want you to have to see me like this."

Like what? she wanted to ask but didn't. "I'll go as soon as they get here. I don't want them to have to hunt me down after I'm halfway home."

Kade nodded. He pressed his back against the wall and then slid downward until he sat on the pavement, hands resting on bent knees.

Elizabeth faced the street.

Patrol cars came into view down the road. Flashing lights grew closer.

"Still have access to those recordings?"

"Yup," Kade said.

Elizabeth watched the officers skirt Kade's truck and park. "Was there anything unusual about the car Henderson picked up that day?"

Kade was silent a moment, as Officer Mackey exited his vehicle. "Nothing I remember. Chevy Chevelle. Super Sport. Emerald green paint. Gorgeous car."

The officer's radio crackled with his status and garbled voices from inside. Elizabeth could picture the officer following the same path she and Kade traced minutes before. From inside, Elizabeth heard Mackey request backup. "Anything stand out from the order itself?"

"Straightforward. Detailing. Minor repairs." Kade had his knees bent, his feet flat on the pavement. "There is one thing."

"Oh?"

"Raj did the work."

"Forgive my ignorance," Elizabeth said. "But what's odd about a mechanic detailing a car?"

Kade picked up a bottle cap, litter in front of the shop. He turned it over in his fingers. "Like many jobs, you work your way up. At a hospital, it's not likely that a doctor is going to take your blood sample and change your catheter. The more skills, the more complex the tasks you do. It's what justifies higher pay."

"I follow you. It's odd because it's like the guy wanted a doctor to give him a sponge bath and apply the Band-Aid."

"Exactly."

"But what about not wanting to trust an amateur? If these cars are as valuable as you say, would people really want a newbie handling their property? Seems reasonable to ask for someone with more experience."

"You have a point. If something gets messed up, sourcing parts for classics can take time. Serious time."

Another patrol car headed their way. Elizabeth turned to Kade. "Before I go, any chance I can see that video again?"

40

Elizabeth scrolled through the easiest, fastest, and most delicious five-minute appetizers for any party. Or so the internet promised. Her thumb flicked up on the phone screen and she failed to register the pictures. She attempted to search for inspiration, but the video of Raj played on repeat through her mind.

"I don't know whether to highlight fruity and chocolatey or earthy with some citrus. Or maybe herbaceous? What do you think?" She handed her phone to Casey.

"I've got an orange and cardamom," Casey said. "How about that?"

Elizabeth looked at her brother. His head was bent over her phone, his thumbs tapping a rapid beat across the screen. "Should we have wine? Or how about we serve soda we get from the gas station?"

"Sounds great," he said.

"Are you even listening? Never mind, I know you weren't. And what are you doing on my phone?"

"My bad. I need help. Danny wants me to go on this ride with his club. I've never sat on a motorcycle, let alone been responsible for propelling myself along on one. I can't search on my phone or he'll know, and I've been thinking about taking lessons. He says it's not that hard, and then I said—"

"I don't need the play-by-play. What I need is for you to be a part of this discussion." Elizabeth heard the edge in her own voice. Alma's keychain made a bulge in the pocket of her shorts. "I'm losing my mind here."

Casey frowned at her. "I understand that it can be difficult witnessing a relationship gone right," he said

"Excuse me?"

"Relying on a partner is a healthy thing. We like to connect. Talk to each other about what's going on."

"What do you know about healthy? You're lying to him about knowing how to ride a motorcycle. You engaged in an extra marital affair for years."

Casey closed his eyes and pinched the bridge of his nose. When he opened his eyes, they were steel colored. His tone matched. "Please don't blame me because you won't let yourself like a guy who is totally available and decent."

"Decent?"

"Yes, he's a good guy. He's been good to you. He is decent to kids, and I don't want to see you mess this up because you're scared."

"I've got more to think about than my hormones." Elizabeth snatched her phone back and crossed her arms. A weak effort to regain control over the conversation.

"Really? Is that what you think I'm doing here?" Casey stood up. "Look, Liz. Leaving you all those years ago is something that will eat at me for the rest of my life. You were only eight, and there was no way to explain to you what I had to do and why and how it had nothing to do with you. I see now the damage that caused."

Elizabeth's mental wall crumbled. She dropped her hands to her sides. "I don't blame you, Casey—"

"I know, but I think subconsciously we get weird when people leave us, even if we know why. I can still see your face when I said goodbye to you. It's stamped on my memory, and I will never forget it. What I did, what Nick did when he cheated on you, that doesn't mean it's what everyone will do. What every man will do. Don't let our mistakes limit your happiness. And don't use looking at some dumb recipes to distract you from getting back there and telling Kade how you feel."

Elizabeth blinked at her brother, stunned by his frank statement.

Casey retrieved Elizabeth's bag from the coat hook and handed it to her. He pressed her phone into her hand and gave her a gentle push toward the door. "Go," he said.

Elizabeth was five miles down the road before her head caught up with her heart. She was on her way to tell a man how she felt about him. Her fears and hopes, laid bare. She would confess everything she'd worked so hard to stuff down inside.

With Nick, her ex, they'd met at a party. Their first date was a basketball game followed by some fumblings in the bedroom, holidays at their parents' houses, and an engagement. While she loved Nick then, and still did to a tiny degree, she knew now that she'd never been in love with him. That hadn't been the consideration. She'd been following the path she thought life meant to take. Girl meets boy. Girl marries boy.

Now, back on the road on her way to confess, she was out of her element. Justin, her fleeting romance from last year, had lit a fire in a dusty hearth. Then, in one night, it was snuffed. Even Corbin had fanned the flames. Her reluctant crush. She had baggage, and it wasn't light.

Kade had relit that fire. He kept the coals warm. His now concentrated presence in her life meant more heat than she had ever known before.

Elizabeth hugged the gentle curves of Highway 87, headed north. A sprinkle of lights dotted the valley in the distance.

Around one bend, her headlights flashed on a group of figures in the road. The trio froze, and their eyes flashed greenish-yellow in the pitch black. She saw spots and legs, fur and fawn.

Elizabeth slammed her foot on the brakes. Her tires screeched, blackened marks in their wake. The car skidded off the side of the road, her front tire hooked over the lip of asphalt.

As her chest heaved from exertion. The deer resumed their trek across the road. One looked back to meet her eyes.

A burgundy sedan pulled up alongside Elizabeth's car and rolled down the passenger side window. A woman with bottle blonde hair, hot pink lipstick, and a vape pen in hand stuck her head out. "Hey, hon, you okay?" In the driver's seat, a man with one front tooth and greasy hair leered at Elizabeth.

Elizabeth willed her pulse to slow. "I'm fine. Thanks."

"Suit yourself, sugar," the woman said, and the pair sped off.

Elizabeth eased back onto the highway, her nerves a jangle of knotted wires. She watched every fence line and copse of trees for the shadows of animals. When the bright lights of the tiny college came into view, she relaxed a little. Deer were less prevalent within the town limits.

As she retraced the streets, Elizabeth relived the better parts of her night. The surprise of the picnic. The flecks of gold in Kade's irises. The warmth of his hand in hers. She considered that relationships consisted of hundreds of memories, many sweet, others bitter.

Kade's shop sign came into focus. She steeled herself for whatever would come. At worst, he could reject her. Tell her he didn't feel that way anymore. She would get back in her car, drive home, and move on with her life. At best...Jo was right. She needed to move forward with something.

But what to do next if he feels the same? One step at a time. As she approached the shop, she could see that all the lights were on. The windows blazed with brightness and two bay doors were up.

Elizabeth slowed her car on approach. From the outside, she could see in. Kade was there. She watched his broad frame bend over a work bench covered in piles of paper. His hair stuck up in odd places, and his shirt was untucked. His disheveled look matched the shop. She was about to pull into the parking lot when movement near the office caught her eye.

From the office door came Becky. She crossed the entry with a thick sheaf of papers in her arms. When she reached Kade, Becky set the new stack on the bench, then stood next to the shop owner. He pointed at something on a page, and she looked over his shoulder. Becky brushed against his arm. Elizabeth swallowed a lump of hurt when she saw Kade look down at the other woman.

Elizabeth's fingers gripped the steering wheel as her palms began to sweat. She'd understood, loud and clear, that Becky had an interest in Kade. Had she missed that the attraction was mutual?

I am a fool, she thought. *A complete and total fool.*

"Dang it," she said, and hit the steering wheel with the fleshy part of her palm. The hatchback's horn let out a furtive bleat and Elizabeth sat up straight. She looked toward the garage.

Both Kade and Becky looked up from their work to peer her way in the dark. Without thinking, Elizabeth shifted into gear and sped off.

Two minutes down the road, her phone rang. From its spot on the passenger seat, she could read the caller ID.

Kade Michaels.

She let it ring.

41

Elizabeth did her best to ignore the voicemail well into the next morning.

A part of her hoped the message would disappear if only she waited it out. She'd taken to leaving her phone across a room. *Out of sight, out of mind.*

Instead, the tiny icon beckoned from afar, chipping away at her resolve. Pressing her to listen to Kade's message. To own what happened that night, look her shame and her anger in the eye, and deal with them.

Elizabeth picked up the phone and unlocked the screen. *Not yet,* she told herself. She abandoned the device on the kitchen counter and lugged a basket of laundry outside to hang on the line.

Casey had only shaken his head when she insisted on the clothesline. He said he'd installed a perfectly good clothes dryer because it was the 21st century. Elizabeth insisted on the option, regardless. She loved the scent of prairie on the sheets, Rhett's tiny socks clipped to the line. Sometimes joy in the little things in life made the harder times more bearable.

Boy and dog tumbled out into the sunshine behind Elizabeth. Leia romped after Rhett who followed a butterfly on its chaotic flight.

Elizabeth lugged the damp clothes on one hip, a bag of clothespins in the other.

The clothesline ran from the corral to a small shed. Elizabeth stuffed a few clothespins in her mouth and set to work. Sheets, socks, and tiny T-shirts went up onto the line. She lost herself in the task as puffy white clouds scuttled by, big blue sky arching overhead. Pillowcases snapped in the breeze.

Rhett and Leia collapsed in a pile of soft earth near the corral. Rhett trailed his finger through the dirt, tracing Leia's paw. Two magpies called out from the barn roof as they surveyed the scene. The blue patches on their wings flashed in the sunshine.

Heat shimmered above the metal surfaces of the corral and barn roof. A trickle of sweat beaded at Elizabeth's collarbone and trickled down her chest. At the bottom of the basket, she found Rhett's swim trunks, a bright Hawaiian scene printed on the fabric. They'd had an afternoon under the sprinkler on Casey's sparse patch of grass. As Elizabeth clipped them into place, last on the line, she had an idea.

Elizabeth ducked into the house to grab her phone. In the city, she would never have left her son alone, not even for a minute. Out here, the fear dissipated, somewhat, some of the time. With scrub brush for miles in every direction, her worry shifted. Especially with a four-legged protector. Within thirty seconds, she was back in the yard.

She bypassed the voicemail and dialed before she could second-guess the decision.

"Elizabeth," Kade said. "I wondered when I'd hear from you."

That voice. Smooth and confident, with a raw edge. Like a hot rod, idling. "Oh?"

"I called you. Left you a message. Didn't you get it?" Sounds of clanging came through the speaker behind Kade. Voices and the whine of an engine followed.

"Nope. No. I mean not yet. Voicemail was invented in the 70s, and I can't say it's improved much. Bet it will come through now that I'm back on the wifi. Must be why everyone texts now."

"So, I need to text you the next time I see your car?"

Elizabeth let a beat go by before she stammered out a reply. "Uh, hmm? You mean if it was ever stolen? I don't think anyone would want to steal my hunk of junk, do you?"

"That's not what I meant. I called—"

She interrupted before he could comment on her car, last night, or why he was there with Becky. "I called because I wanted to see if you and Benny would like to meet us at the pool. Jo told me all about it. Biggest one around, fed by snow runoff. Shallow end for the littles. Snack bar. I can't think of anything better on a hot day than a dip and a snow cone. What do you think?"

Elizabeth waited, out of breath, for him to reply. In her mind, the request was innocent, another exposure to the illusion of a family. A unit. Maybe after she dwelled in the bliss of togetherness, she would attempt to sort out what she'd seen.

"That sounds really great—"

"Great. I can be ready in—"

"But—"

"But?" The vision of Rhett and Benny playing on the splash pad, she and Kade stretched out on towels, drowsy from the pool, nachos, and afternoon rays, popped like a bubble burst.

"I can't today. I've got a big to-do list. Too much going on over here."

"Oh? Oh. I'm sorry, I forgot. I should have stayed to help you clean up last night."

"Well, yes. No. Uh. I'm just...busy."

The stumble of his words wounded her. Why wouldn't he tell her what he was up to? *What is he hiding?* "I see."

"You could take Benny, though," Kade said, his voice urgent, apologetic. "He'd love it, I'm sure. He's over at Marg's house. He doesn't know how to swim, though. His mom didn't teach him yet..."

Elizabeth knew better than most what didn't get taught when one's mother was locked up behind bars. She frowned, her thoughts snagged on all that was taken from Benny. All that had been taken from her.

Kade continued, "He's got trunks at home and those floaty things. You know, the arm donuts?"

"Sure," Elizabeth said. She attempted to pitch cheer into her reply. "I'll do that. Rhett would love to have a friend along." *As would I.*

42

Elizabeth eased her hatchback alongside the gas pump and shifted into park. In the back, Benny read from a book on volcanoes. He paused to point to pictures, turning the book toward Rhett.

Rhett was strapped in his seat next to Benny, an eager listener. She'd rolled down the windows while at the pump. Rhett had brought his seal figurine along for the ride, the only aquatic animal in his growing menagerie. Eddie Enos, their friend who lived in Hawaii, had given it to Rhett when they'd met at Christmas. Her son moved the plastic animal along the window ledge in waves. Elizabeth worried Rhett would drop the seal into the asphalt ocean below. "I'm going to pump the gas, so can Mr. Seal swim inside the car where it's safe?"

Her son blinked at her, then returned to his play. *He's only been talking for a few months, Liz,* she told herself. *Some grown adults don't say much, either.*

Elizabeth lived a daily struggle of trying to figure out what was normal for him. Rhett's speech had been delayed until well after two years old and was still slow to come. Rhett spoke—or didn't speak—on his own terms. Do too much to influence the situation and she risked frustrating him and stalling growth. Do too little and she risked not providing extra care. It was an endless cycle of worry and anxiety. Was this a given part of mothering?

Examples of motherhood mixed in her mind and heart. Her own mother had been hands off, reluctant to tell Elizabeth much of anything, let alone essentials. As an adult, Elizabeth saw her mother as a flawed human. A victim of abuse. Jo was almost the opposite. For a woman whose life had not been blessed with her own children, she counted half of the county as her honorary brood. Many a Sunday Supper held a table full of those Jo had mothered. *How are we all not a combination of the mothering we give and receive?*

While the gas flowed into her tiny car, the dollars adding up, Elizabeth checked in on Rhett. When she made the face of a monkey, her cheeks puffed and ears stretched out, Rhett said, "Monk!"

I'll take that as a win, Elizabeth thought.

"He's cute," Alma said. The woman approached, a staple gun in one hand and a stack of fliers in the other. "Getting bigger every time I see him."

"Thanks. I think so, but I have an obvious bias." Elizabeth addressed her son. "Rhett, do you remember Alma? Both of you love animals very much."

Alma waved at Rhett. "Hello, nice to see you again."

In greeting, Rhett held out the seal to Alma. "See," he said, in explanation.

"Cool seal," Alma said. "You have good taste."

"Oh, hey," Elizabeth said. She reached through the driver's side window and grabbed her purse. "I found this the other night. Thought it might be yours."

When she saw what Elizabeth held, Alma's face pinched in confusion. "I've been looking for that. Where did you find it?" She pocketed the keychain.

"In the park, after the concert. I figured you must know one of the musicians or something."

"I do...well, I did, but..." Her mouth formed silent words, muttering to herself. "I had a spare but this saved me, thanks."

Elizabeth unlatched the pump from her car and hung it back into place. "What are you up to? Most people at the gas station bring a car. I've heard the classics can be gas guzzlers."

"They are but I'm not most people—at least not today. I've got some fliers to hang up for the car show, drum up some more attendees."

"Is the Tardis ready?"

"Getting there. We'll see what I can finish. I've got overtime this week, and we still have cars to finish. I'm also filming some promos for Kade. You know, B-reel stuff he can use for socials."

Elizabeth tore off the receipt from the machine and shoved it in her pocket. "I'm impressed. I thought Kade had more than enough business, though."

"He didn't tell you?"

"Tell me what?"

Alma transferred the papers to the other arm. She looked around. Two pumps over, a woman in a caftan pumped gas into a sedan. Next to her, a handful of teenagers piled out of a sedan, headed for the little store. "Rumors. People think he's got something shady going on. That Raj wasn't some freak accident. People don't want to visit a shop that's full of criminals—or amateurs. Not that we have any of those left anymore, either. Besides me, I guess. I'm lucky Kade didn't fire me after the break-in. Now the college wants to review their contract with him. Said they have some *concerns.* Kade is taking it pretty hard. The whole program was Raj's baby."

Elizabeth recalled the phone call, the worry in Kade's voice. Had he been too ashamed to tell her? There was so much she didn't yet know about him, about the stressors he faced in his business. How could she date him—if that's what they were doing—and not take the time to get to know him at that level?

"Anyway," Alma continued. "He's holed up in his office going over everything with you-know-who between cars. He sent me out with these since we're waiting on the parts delivery." She waved the fliers in the air. "Once I'm done hanging them, I'm off for the day, which isn't a bad thing. I could use the break. It's hot."

"How do you feel about nachos?"

43

Cumulus clouds formed one circus animal and then another. A lion shifted into an elephant and then an ostrich before turning into a dragon that consumed them all.

Elizabeth lay on her back on a towel she'd spread across the stubbled grass, sunglasses anchored over the bridge of her nose. She'd applied sunscreen in liberal layers over her skin and stretched into the warmth.

Tasked with occupying the boys, Elizabeth had tugged on a tankini covered in monstera leaves. She'd tossed on a cover-up and packed the car with every possible need for the afternoon. Floaties, plastic boats, spare suits, and change for the snack bar. She and Rhett had picked Benny up from the Harts' ranch and headed south.

Running into Alma was a bonus. Elizabeth barely had time to unfurl the towels before the Tardis slid into the parking spot next to her hatchback. Alma waved from the car, extracted a bag from the back, and joined them under the trees.

The Buffalo pool was bigger than a basketball court and crawling with children. Diving boards lined the deep end. A rotating line of swimmers dove into the pool's depths from varying heights. The tiniest of jumpers executed a perfect cannonball, sending up an eruption of water. At the shallow end, babies in ruffled hats and swim diapers splashed among their caretakers who sat in the water, chatting.

Alma volunteered to take the boys into the water. She held Rhett's hand as he inched down the ramp, adjusting to the frigid water. He'd brought his plastic seal and held it out to his newest friend for acknowledgement. Alma used her hand to mime swimming along the waves. Benny floated nearby, his bright green plastic goggles magnifying his eyes. He watched a group of boys clamber over each other to snatch a basketball. The winner aimed for the hoop attached to the pool.

For the moment, Elizabeth was alone. She whipped out her phone to scroll down the screen. With a few taps of her thumb, she revealed a wealth of information.

Social media was sparse, but present. Pictures with high school buddies. A golfing fundraiser and a post selling an old television stand. Nothing stood out. Elizabeth kept hunting.

Next, she found a blog detailing sponsorship of an all-girls eco car team, champions for two years running. There was a donor line to an extracurricular program at a city school. A graduation from community college and a finishers list for a 10K race.

With the last click, she found something that caused her to sit upright and block the glare from her screen.

In an article from a California newspaper, she saw him. Raj.

The headline was telling, the paragraph even more so. Details from a night with a group of other teens. Breaking and entering, a convenience store. Possession with intent to sell. A second gas station. Then drug court for youths at risk.

Raj had a criminal record.

44

"I made him wear sunscreen, and I limited him to three sugary snacks. Two if you don't count liquids."

Elizabeth stood under the open bay door. She spoke to Kade's legs. The pair stuck out from under a Saab. Elizabeth considered them not unlike those of the Wicked Witch of the East, and she snickered.

"I'm sure he loved every moment of it. He's been nagging me to take him ever since he heard about the place."

"He seemed okay in the water, but we didn't let him go far." Benny stuck close to the adults, but he'd kicked a few circles to avoid the shrieking kids playing Marco Polo. When Elizabeth waved him in for snacks, he paddled straight to her. His scrawny arms and legs propelled him through the water.

There was a *clink clank* from under the car before Kade replied. "Natural born, likely. His mom could swim like a fish. At the lake. We used to spend every summer day in an old canoe. Lunch was a bag of white bread and a jar of peanut butter—if we were lucky. Wouldn't have it any other way, though. Kids don't get that kind of fun anymore. Thanks for taking him."

"I'm hoping to give a little of that to Rhett, living here. I'll have to get him out to the lake."

Kade said nothing from under the car. *Clink.* In the office, Benny had Rhett in the rolling chair. He spun the younger boy in a slow circle. Rhett gripped the sides of the chair, mouth open in excitement.

"I found something on Raj."

Clank. Bang. "Ow!" Kade rolled out from under the car, one hand to his forehead.

"Ice?"

Kade pointed. "In that little freezer."

Elizabeth wrapped the ice pack in a clean shop towel and handed it to Kade. He pressed the pack to his head while she told him what she'd found. "So, it looks like he was into some things as a kid. He got into big trouble, cleaned up, and went on to be a great human being."

"How did you find all this?"

"The internet." Elizabeth shrugged.

"Huh. I've got to kick this around in my brain a bit before I can layer it over the Raj I knew."

Elizabeth nodded. "Well, the boys had a blast today—and so did Alma."

"Alma?"

Elizabeth fluffed at her damp hair with her hand. The chlorine left it lank and wavy as it dried. "She finished your posters and came to the pool. Pretty sure she's my son's first crush."

Kade's mouth twisted up into a grin. "Oh, really?"

"She's great. I hope you keep her."

Kade lowered the ice pack from his head and looked around the shop. "At this rate, I couldn't afford to get rid of her even if she wasn't great with the wrench. As it is, I could only give her the afternoon off. She's been pulling nights to help out. Going to make a fortune in overtime."

"Don't mess it up," Elizabeth said. "I think I have a new friend."

"Speaking of friends, you look hot with wet hair."

Elizabeth pitched an eyebrow upward and crossed her arms. "Do you say that to all your friends?"

"Only those I want to become much more than that."

45

Cherry-chocolate swirl dripped down the back of Elizabeth's hand. The melted ice cream snaked around her wrist. Before she could think twice, she licked the droplet and then the lip of the cone.

Kade watched her, staring.

"What?"

Kade shook his head, as if to dislodge a thought. "If Benny does that kind of thing, I send him to the kitchen to wash up. But you..."

Elizabeth's cheeks pinked. In these moments, when it was the two of them, Kade was flirtatious, playful. This was in stark contrast to the gruff exterior he'd shared when they'd met. Back then, he was her date's enemy.

Now, he was her date.

Alma had threatened to lock him out if he didn't get some fresh air and something other than coffee in his system. He'd invited Elizabeth to escape with him for a cone and a walk.

"She's got Benny sorting parts. He loves polishing, too. Poor kid has been watching more TV this week than ever before, and unlike most kids, that's not his thing."

"I bet you're looking forward to the end of the show. Things can settle back to normal."

Kade was quiet, thoughtful. He took another lick of his mint chocolate chip. "Actually, I'm not."

Elizabeth tucked her arm in his. They'd parked near the ice cream stand, avoiding the band shell. When the bored teen behind the counter presented their cones, Elizabeth offered a taste to Kade. He'd followed suit. Was ice cream the way to tip toe into a relationship when the backstory of both people was so...heavy? "That surprises me."

"It's just that once all of this dies down, it'll hit me."

Elizabeth swallowed, dared to ask. "What's that?"

"Raj. I've been so busy I've hardly had time to eat solid food let alone let the truth sink in. What am I going to do? Alma is great but it's like she has to dance around me, worried I'm falling apart. Which I kind of am. Like a landmine in a field next to which you have to build a house. I miss my colleague, my friend. I'm a mess."

Loss. So much of life centered on losing, whether it be time, money, or loved ones. Elizabeth wondered at all the effort gone into this cycle of sadness. No wonder ice cream existed. Fast cars, kids, and puppies.

"Missing people can be an incredible ache," she said. "Not sure I'm good at what to do with that pain myself."

"Having you here is helpful. Having you care enough about what happened to dig up information on Raj's past is helpful. I left a message at his mom's place in California. Hoping she'll call me back. I have some questions."

"Do you speak to her a lot?"

"No, but I should. Raj would yammer on and on about that woman like she hung the moon. Said she was there for him when no one else wanted to deal with his teenage self. Now I know a little depth behind that statement."

Elizabeth hugged Kade's arm with her own. She took her first bite of the cone lip, a satisfying crunch that revealed more ice cream behind.

They'd skirted the edge of the park and headed uphill along a tall chain-link fence. On the other side of the barrier, tall grasses, yellowed in the summer heat, swayed in the evening breeze. Large signs posted every few feet forbade visitors from feeding the animals.

"Color me curious," she said. "But what's behind the fence?"

Without following her gaze, Kade said, "You'll see."

When they crested the top of Highland Avenue, Elizabeth sucked in her breath. Thunderclouds rolled dark over the prairie to the north, blackening against the growing twilight. Golden fields contrasted the inky, navy sky, and farms dotted the landscape. Lights in town winked on, and the hum of summer insects fought with the night birds' calls. First one bat darted through the air, and then another chased behind. The world was on a precipice, balanced on the brink of evening.

"Turn around," Kade said.

Elizabeth did as he asked. There, on the hill behind the fence, several walnut and cream humps took shape. Elizabeth watched as one shifted, lifting a head with a massive rack of antlers. The animal chewed a wad of grass as it observed them from a distance. "Wow," she said, a soft utterance.

"Takes my breath away every time," Kade said. He stood behind her, so close she could feel his breath on the back of her neck. He pointed over her shoulder toward another spot within the enclosure. Mountains of brown, shaggy hair moved in a group, their heavy heads and small eyes unconcerned by the visitors. A smaller version, reddish, gamboled alongside.

"Bison *bison*," she said. "Easiest scientific name to remember."

"And their red dog baby."

"As a mom, it's hard to imagine hauling around a seventy-plus pound baby, but yeah, they are super cute."

They watched the herd move down the hill to a barn-like structure to bed down for the night. Hoofprint after hoofprint, the massive animals moved across the ground as though it were a sea and they, its swimmers. The youngest kicked about among them, a child protesting bedtime.

"He seems to listen well enough," Elizabeth said. "At least, he's headed in the direction of bed. Maybe Rhett wouldn't mind a fur brother to go with his fur sister."

"Speaking of listening," Kade said, then popped the end of his cone into his mouth. He chewed for a moment, then gestured for their walk to continue. "Benny's therapy has been going well."

"That's good news," Elizabeth said. She wondered what her life might have been like if she'd had therapy when her own mother went to prison. "I bet that will make a world of difference."

"It has. And not just because of Polly. Benny is a different kid. Learns differently. Having someone other than me to talk to about stuff has been helpful." Kade turned his head to meet her eye.

Elizabeth nodded. "Therapy can be great for kids. Give them another cheerleader on their team."

"Have you and...uh, Nick...thought about therapy for Rhett?"

They neared the park again. Their path followed a sidewalk opposite where the stage loomed in the dark. While she couldn't see it, it was as if the moment called to her in the night. The past pressed on her in the moment, the weight of judgment she hadn't seen coming.

"No, why would we?"

"I don't know." Kade lifted a shoulder and dropped it, a casual acknowledgement. "Maybe because Rhett has gone through some stuff. He might think differently too."

"He can't talk, Kade." Elizabeth released his arm. Turned to face him. A pit of irritation bubbled up from somewhere deep inside. The emotion threatened to morph into a solid form. "How would therapy help if he can't talk?"

"Okay, okay. I thought—"

The bubbling intensified, Elizabeth brimming with a bitter tang in her mouth. "You thought what? That I wouldn't have thought of that myself? That a teacher wouldn't have considered therapy? Or that I wouldn't want that for my own son? Nice, Kade."

"I'm sorry, I just—"

"You know, the ice cream was great. I think it's time for you to go back to work and for me to go home to my son. That's what sacrifice for the boy I love looks like. Maybe you should check your priorities before you go around telling others what to do."

Elizabeth stomped off to her car, flung open the door, and slumped into the seat. She hated that the engine turned over once before roaring to life. When she backed out, her brakes screeched. She tried to ignore the master mechanic, staring in her wake.

46

Too fast, too much, and too soon. These were the excuses that pounded a rhythm through Elizabeth's thoughts. Like a record, they spun until she was dizzy with regret.

She'd wished the words back about two miles down the road. At two a.m. her brain refused a return to sleep, preferring to fixate on the exact moment she'd fouled up the date. What gave everyone permission to point out your failures in a constant stream of feedback?

Kade could be right. Rhett might benefit from therapy. Nick had suggested as much, and Elizabeth said she'd consider. She was just a mother tired of being told by almost everyone she knew all the ways she could be better. Should be better.

Mixed in with the self-pity was a dose of shame for the way she'd treated Kade. He'd intended to help, to share something that made a difference, and she'd snapped.

What she should have said was, "Thank you for thinking of him." Or "Nick and I are already checking out our options." Even "That's pretty personal for me to hear right now," would have been a better option. Instead, she'd had an opportunity and blew it.

"Esprit d'escalier," she said aloud.

The customer ahead of her in line claimed their macchiato and left. Elizabeth was exposed, talking to herself. Gary, the barista on duty, waited for her order. "Not sure I know that one."

"Sorry," she said. "I was lost in my thoughts. I'll take my usual."

"Dirty chai, it is. What is it, by the way?" Gary ran the grinder, then measured espresso into the portafilter. He pressed on the grounds with the tamper. He spun one finger in a loop through the air. "That thing you just said."

"Hmm? Oh. It's French. It means the 'spirit of the stairs.'"

Gary hooked the portafilter into the machine and pressed a button. A whirring sounded from deep within its bowels. Coffee dripped into the ceramic cup below. "Some kind of cocktail? Racehorse?"

"It refers to when you're in an argument but don't think of the right response to someone until you've left."

Gary lifted a carafe of milk up to the steamer wand. "I got you. Like when you want to replay the ending so you can change it."

"Hadn't thought about it that way, but yeah."

"You're on the stairs, aren't you?" Gary handed her a warm cup.

The scent of cinnamon filled her nostrils. "I am."

"Must have missed the metaphor," Alma said. She breezed in through the door and approached the counter. "Cold brew, please. Splash of cream."

Gary held a glass under the tap and filled it to within an inch of the top.

"New favorite," Alma said to Elizabeth and held up the glass. "Late nights at the shop mean afternoon caffeine."

"That'd give me the shakes for hours. How's business?"

Alma took a sip. A creamy mustache lined her upper lip. She closed her eyes for a moment and smiled. "Heaven."

"Remind me to switch careers."

Alma snorted. "Oh no, the shop is a wreck. People waited until the last minute to bring in their cars. Plus, whatever construction they're doing on Loucks sent in four people with popped tires. I'd send them a thank you note if it were the slow season but today, it's madness. Plus, my boss has a bee in his bonnet, as my aunt would say. Or is it don't poke the bear?" Alma paused to take another sip. Her pink tongue erased cream from her lips. "So, he's a volcano, ready to blow, and Becky keeps hovering around him asking what she can do. It's 'Oh, Kade,' this and 'What do you think about that?' Makes me want to puke."

"You're right. Having someone cater to your every need is vomitous," Gary said, snark on the edge of his voice.

"You know what I mean," Alma said. "It's too much. Like I don't even see her do anything with all that paperwork. She's always watching him work. I even caught her stuffing some of the files in her purse, rather than filing them."

"Wait, what?" Jealousy creeped up Elizabeth's spine like a boa constrictor. That the woman continued to fawn over Kade was one thing, and nothing new. That she slacked at her supposed job was another.

"You caught her?" Gary used the glass cleaner to rinse the carafe. "What'd she say?"

Alma nodded. "Red handed. Said she was taking them home to double check the numbers. She put them back, pretending she'd changed her mind and would be too busy."

Elizabeth frowned, holding her cup to her lips. She tapped a finger against the side, thinking. "Did you see which files she'd taken?"

"You think she's hiding state secrets at the garage of a local grease monkey?" Gary tilted his chin, considering. "Could make for good television."

"I don't know," Elizabeth said. "Just curious if there was a reason."

"Not sure, but I could check. When I caught her, she tossed them on top of a file cabinet and told Kade she'd be back after lunch."

Gary added Alma's tip to the jar. "Keep me posted if you find out," he teased. "It's not every day you get to hear an accounting mystery."

Elizabeth laughed along with Gary and Alma, but she was already lost in thought. Why would Becky go out of her way with a pile of old files? *Why won't she leave Kade alone?*

47

"Please let me apologize before you say anything else," Elizabeth said.

"Can I say hello?" Kade stood in the doorway of his shop. He wiped at both hands with a rag.

"No. I mean, yes. Of course." Elizabeth pressed her lips together, wishing her nerves to still. "Hello."

"Hi." The corner of Kade's mouth twitched, as if he had yet to decide how he felt about her intrusion.

Elizabeth took a deep breath. Her chest heaved on the inhale. She shifted her feet, then interlaced her fingers for the exhale. "I wasn't stalking you the other night. Well. I guess I was, but only for about thirty seconds, and that was an accident. I mean, not that it was an accident that I was watching you but that I didn't know I'd be watching you. Or rather, I didn't set out to do that."

"You didn't plan to drive here?" Kade waved a hand toward the shop at large.

"No, I did. But not to watch. To talk. You know. About us."

Kade raised an eyebrow. "Go on."

Elizabeth hesitated and pressed the tips of her thumbs together. "When I got here, it was clear you were...busy. It hit me that while I was so focused on you and me and how I felt and what I wanted you to understand about me, you'd been broken into and were here working. What I wanted to say seemed selfish, like I was interrupting a really awful evening to make everything about me and my feelings. So, I didn't want to bother you. Then, when you didn't want to go to the pool—" Elizabeth barreled ahead, without catching her breath. She didn't want to picture Kade with Becky again. "I thought you didn't...that you were...Well. You didn't tell me much, so I didn't know what to think. Then, when you invited me to get ice cream, I was confused all over again. At the park when you said that I should, well...I was already a bit of a wreck, and I thought—"

"You thought I was commenting on you as a parent."

The remaining air whooshed out of Elizabeth's lungs in relief. "Yeah. To be honest, I did. I'm sensitive about that. I'd say it's part of motherhood, but I don't want to leave out fathers or anyone else, so maybe it's about doing right by the kid in your life. I'm sensitive to criticism, I admit it. Rhett is the most precious person I'll ever know, the person I will love more than anyone else in this world, and I don't like the idea that I might not do everything right for him. That I won't be the perfect mother he deserves. Even the thought of that breaks my heart, no matter how much I tell myself I'm a decent mom. That these feelings are normal. I didn't want to hear that message from you, too. Even though I know that's not what you meant, that you were trying to help. It's that I am doing my best, and somehow that will never be enough, no matter what."

Her chin fell to her chest. Emotions spent, she gathered herself for his reaction.

"Come with me."

48

Kade took her hand and began to walk.

"Where are we going?"

"Downtown," he said.

"Shouldn't you lock up?"

"Alma's there." His answer was quick, unconcerned. Elizabeth looked back at the garage windows, curious if Becky, too, was there.

They crossed Broadway and turned down First Street. At night, the vintage brick buildings loomed overhead. Their history, a century in the making, held court alongside the buildings, as though structures had a soul.

Named for a Union general in the Civil War, Sheridan was established by a man who became its first postmaster. He envisioned a town in the beautiful valley near Goose Creek. The new residents welcomed the railroad and what they envisioned as progress. Ranching, agriculture, and mining launched the popularity of the new county. As the next century brought change, growth slowed, leaving Wyoming one of the biggest, yet the least populated, states.

Fine by me, Elizabeth thought.

On a short bridge that spanned Big Goose Creek, Kade paused to look out over the water.

A car zipped by, the windows open. Creedence Clearwater Revival drifted out the window, like the train of a fancy gown.

"I come here to think, sometimes," Kade said.

Elizabeth waited for more. When nothing came, she ventured a comment. "It's different, but I can see the appeal."

She peered over the dented guardrail into the water. A man-made channel directed the creek through town. Soft ripples textured the surface. The water was shallow, sided by cement, and otherwise unadorned. This was in stark contrast to the places where the creek meandered with freedom, trees its canopy. "It's...efficient."

Streetlight reflected on the surface of the water. Streaks of golden light with the occasional shimmering neon stripe. "It reminds me that we can intervene, divert, plan, and reconfigure. But that which was here long before us will continue to exist long after. It's like an ego check, you know?" Kade turned his back to the railing and leaned into a dented spot. The path of a car collision made plain in the metal.

"Like we can pretend, and even fight, to be in control of our lives. But there's so much more to it."

"Something like that," Kade said, gnawing at the inside of his cheek. "It's also a reminder for me to slow down. Trust, have faith. If I do that—understand that the best things in life are a marathon, not a sprint—I can find my patience. Find my strength."

Elizabeth stared out over the water. Why did it feel as though this moment with Kade was exactly what she needed to hear? She nodded, a slow acknowledgment. "I've put so much pressure on myself to launch a business and be an instant success that I forget all the work I did just to get through today. It's not just about me being a mom, it's about me being a human. Trying to make something of myself."

Kade nodded. "Short of winning the lottery, most things we do are a ton of work. When they actually work out, sometimes we miss that. We're already focused on the next thing."

"Like a footnote you don't stop to read."

"Yeah, like that."

Elizabeth waited for her go-to stream of facts to take over. Waited for the urge to tell Kade about the first footnote, the average length of a footnote, or some other rushed fact. Her brain was mush, though. A soft, drowsy, peaceful place. For the moment. "I can be more upfront with my heart, my goals. I am working my tush off, and I want so much out of life. I need to allow myself that dream. And others."

"You can share them with me," Kade said. "I've got a few of my own."

"Okay," Elizabeth said. She inhaled and exhaled, a deliberate breath. "I want my own business. By that, I don't mean that I have to be alone—I've been working on that, too—but that I am my own boss. I want my son to be proud of all I've accomplished. Be proud I'm his mom."

"I'd put money on the fact that he already is. I have it on good authority as a son, myself." Kade turned back to the water, resting his forearms on the guardrail, and continued. "I can respect those dreams. You work hard for what you want. I'm smart enough not to get in the way of a determined woman."

"I'll try not to run you over."

Kade laughed, "Fair. But I have some dreams, too."

Elizabeth laced her fingers together. The breeze lifted the fine hair on her arms. A chill played across the back of her neck. Stars blinked overhead, their twins pooled in the water below. "You in the mood for sharing?"

"I think I need to. I want Benny to grow up as healthy and happy as someone can, given all the cards he's holding. I want to be there for his Civics Bee tournaments, school dances, and all his graduations. I want him to feel okay about who he is, know that he is loved, very much, even if some of his family didn't know how to do that right."

"He's an incredible kid."

"He is." Kade reached for her hand and held it. He looked into her eyes. "I want to grow my business. Maybe open a shop in Billings. Specialize. Alma has me thinking about a restoration side, something more formal. Detailed. A place where I can use a little more of my creative side. She says people have to find somewhere to put their creative impulses or they suffer."

"Wise words from someone her age. I haven't fully learned that lesson myself."

Kade didn't crack a smile. Instead, he squeezed her hand. "There's more. I don't want to do it all alone." Kade watched her, his eyes searching hers for meaning.

Elizabeth broke his gaze to look left, then right. Anywhere and everywhere other than the intensity of his stare. When she'd regathered her confidence, she lifted her eyes again. "Okay. Say you were to try on that dream. To see if it fits. How would you know?"

Kade cocked his chin. "What's with teachers asking the tough questions?"

Elizabeth shrugged. "Can't help it."

"All right," he said. "I'd be looking for something that felt natural."

"What is that supposed to mean?"

"Cotton vs. polyester, you know? I get that these things take work, but if there's a lot of friction—itching, you know? Then it's not right."

"Are you going to hold up your side of the laundry?" Elizabeth lifted an eyebrow.

Kade crossed his arms. "Reasonable question. Yeah, I plan to. I'm not always the...uh...easiest person. Especially before my coffee—"

"Same," Elizabeth said, the corner of her mouth tilting up.

Kade's tone dropped, and he kept talking. "And let's be honest. With Benny and everything...I've got some complications others don't have. I'm still a work in progress."

"Me, too."

"I've also been doing my own thing for long enough that I think heavy oversight would freak me out."

"Oversight?"

"Oh, I don't know. Drive by viewings of my whereabouts..."

"I didn't mean—" Elizabeth bit her lip. Shame washed over her again. If they were going anywhere—together—she had a few requirements of her own. "I apologize for that. It won't happen again. Which leads me to one of my requirements."

"Oh?"

"We let the past be the past."

"Can do. Letting it go as I speak."

"And, like you," Elizabeth started, "I've got a little boy who means more to me than anyone else. That has to be respected."

Kade nodded, clear agreement. "Number one."

"Oh, and you have to like my beer. And Casey's cheese."

"I can respect these things. When do we start?"

49

Elizabeth slung a beer over Kade's shoulder, he accepted. She then rounded the couch to plop down on the pile of pillows. She set her own bottle on a coaster, then slid a second cork disk over to Kade.

With a wink, Casey claimed prior plans with a video game and retired to his room. Every few minutes an, "Aww, man!" came from behind the door. He brother liked to play live with other players around the globe. Otherwise, she and Kade were alone. Benny and Rhett were tucked into twin sleeping bags on the floor of the spare bedroom, Leia sprawled on top. The boys had jumped at the chance for a slumber party. Elizabeth wasn't sure how she'd make it over to her own bed, but that was a problem for later.

Now, Kade was in her living room. And, they may have committed to maybe being together. A real couple.

"This is heaven," Kade said. He spread another cracker with goat cheese. "I didn't get to try any at the party."

"You were a little occupied."

"I was," he said.

Elizabeth lifted her bottle. "To Raj."

Kade clinked the neck of his bottle against hers. "To Raj."

"Any news on that front?"

"None yet." Kade peeled at the label on his bottle.

Elizabeth pressed buttons on the remote. She'd suggested he bring Benny. Stay for a movie and a couple of beers. It was a safe date. With Casey home and the boys in the other room, Elizabeth had set the stage for togetherness. Baby steps.

The news popped on screen. A man in a suit spoke to the camera. The sound was down, but Elizabeth knew the type. Confidence, too much vocabulary. Spoke without actually saying much of substance. "What are we in the mood for?" She consulted the remote.

"Hang on," Kade said. "Could you turn it up? I think they're talking about the car show."

Elizabeth pressed the volume button. The sound came up, and the man was still talking. She cast a glance back at the bedroom doors.

"...this weekend. The show draws thousands from all over who convene to see an outstanding selection of cars. They have everything from the casual garage hound to the professional detailer. No matter your decade, there's a car for you. We interviewed one of the sponsors last week."

A man filled the frame. Elizabeth recognized him in an instant. Salt and pepper hair swept away from his face. A Florida tan. The man from the video she'd watched dozens of times.

The newscaster held a foam-topped microphone with both hand s."Mr. Henderson, anything special in store for us this year?"

"You know me. I wouldn't bring anything less." The man smiled a jack-o-lantern grin at the camera.

"I love it. Guess we'll have to attend to see them. Word on the street is that you are revealing something special at the show."

"That I am. I have a new business venture for the classic automotive community, and I can't wait to share it with you all."

"Before we go, any comment on the attack of a local mechanic?"

"Turn that up," Kade said. He looked at Elizabeth. "Please."

She handed him the remote. He pressed a button and the volume notched upward.

"...so I can't comment on that case."

"Well, folks, you heard it here first..."

Elizabeth stared at the screen. Over Guy's shoulder, another face came in and out of view. The person at his right elbow came into view in profile.

A dark curl of hair over his right ear. The lacework of exposed tattoos poking out from a sleeve. Elizabeth recognized the person as though he wore a crown of gilded olive leaves around his head.

Kade held up the remote, as if to change the channel.

"Wait, don't!" She shouted this at the screen, louder than she should have. "Look!"

Kade squinted at the screen. "That's—"

"Thor!"

"But," Kade said, his brain catching up with the screen, "he'd quit. Right after the party. I figured he was spooked."

"Looks like he'd found a new boss."

50

Elizabeth slipped between cars, each fancier than the next. She tracked Kade ahead of her by the shuffle of his boots. Kade glanced at the dash of each vehicle he passed, his frown deepening at each pause.

"What are we looking for?" Elizabeth whispered, unsure of how close the security guard paced.

"I'll know it when I see it," he answered, not bothering to lower his voice.

Kade's confidence did little to soothe her nerves. Sneaking among expensive assets, peering into private property, would raise the eyebrows of many.

Elizabeth had met Kade downtown for the annual Drive In. He'd explained that the night before the show, many of the car owners parked their cars ahead of time. The WYO Theater projected a classic movie on its north wall, and people gathered outside to watch. This way, owners avoided pre-show traffic. A couple of temporary security guards patrolled the street.

Elizabeth saw the edge of the movie projected above the row of cars. Figures flickered across the makeshift screen. When she looked back, she'd lost sight of Kade. She ducked around a Packard and stooped below its fender when one of the night's guards strolled by the shoe shop. She counted to ten before sticking her head out to search for her accomplice.

"I found one!" Kade whisper-shouted from across the street. "Look!"

Elizabeth snuck over to join him. He pointed at a handwritten card propped underneath the windshield. On manila cardstock, someone had printed the make, model, and year of each car, followed by its owner. The car in question had Henderson Classics printed in blue ink. "His company?"

Kade nodded. "Any of those belong to Guy. We did the work on many, if not most of them. I called Becky to see if I could get a list, but she didn't pick up. I left a message. Meanwhile, I should recognize most of them."

"Okay, then let's keep track of what we find. If Becky calls you back—"

"When."

"When Becky calls you back, we can zero in. Look for anything that might be a pattern."

They split up, Elizabeth taking the east side of the street. Kade took the west. She scribbled information on the back of her hand with a pen, not wanting to risk the light of her phone.

Down the street, the makeshift speakers amplified an argument between the hero and his heroine on screen. He wanted to take to the open road, she wanted to raise a family behind a white picket fence. *Barf,* thought Elizabeth. Then a flash of kelly green caught her eye across Main—Kade's T-shirt. Here she was, scoffing at big screen romance, when she'd needed little to convince her boyfriend—she was still getting used to that term—to hunt for unknown clues in the dark with security guards on the prowl. If this wasn't her kind of romance, she didn't know what was.

Elizabeth passed over a Mercedes, a Jaguar, and a Volkswagen. Those cars came from Thermopolis, Jackson Hole, and one from Boise. Hobby cars. Most of the parked machines were the weekend hobby of a working person who poured their heart, soul, and many dollars into their cars. Elizabeth spotted more than one pair of fuzzy dice, billiard ball shifter knobs, and dash toys. People's personalities came out in their cars, if only one stopped to look.

Elizabeth pictured her own car. Messy, yes, but comfortable. Crayon blue paint. French fries crammed between the seats. A twenty slipped into the glove box in case she ran low on gas.

The glove box.

Kade snuck over and whispered behind her. "Hey—"

Elizabeth swallowed a yelp. When she trusted herself to speak, she whispered, "Pretty sure I almost gave us away. One second while I stuff my heart back in my chest."

"I found it. The Ford 40. Four down, that way." He pointed up the street.

"Is it unlocked?"

51

They crab-walked along the sidewalk, lunging behind parked cars at the slightest sound. The guards looped the cars, a rotation on repeat. Elizabeth and Kade watched as one whistled to the other and the two met in the middle of the street. Silent and still, Elizabeth and Kade watched the pair chat. One pointed toward the screen, the other nodded, and the first headed toward the crowd.

"Almost there," Kade mouthed, then pointed north. They moved away from the guards and the light.

Kade stopped at the back of the Ford. Elizabeth beheld the cherry red paint. The smell of wax, fresh leather, and tire cleaner filled her nostrils.

"Try the door," she whispered. Their plan, should they be caught, was to have Kade claim he'd left a tool in one of the vehicles.

Kade nodded, then approached the door panel. He scouted the street, then wrapped his hands around the handle. He pulled in one quick yank and—nothing.

His mouth formed the word she'd feared. "Locked."

Elizabeth risked a peek in the passenger-side window. Creamy interior gleamed in the moonlight, chrome detailing throughout.

"Dang," she whispered, then something caught her eye.

The glovebox. The corner of an envelope stuck out from the compartment, a blemish against the spotless cream interior.

Elizabeth tapped Kade on the shoulder and pointed at the window. Kade peered in the car, and his eyes went wide. His hands extracted the phone from his pocket, and he flicked on the flashlight.

"What do you think you're doing?"

A flashlight beam scraped across Elizabeth and Kade. The security guard was back, flashlight held at his shoulder.

Kade stood and brushed his hands off on his jeans. He reached out a hand to Elizabeth to offer a boost. "What do you mean?"

"You're sneaking around cars in the dark. You tell me."

"Sneaking? No one is sneaking. I'm checking on my cars." Kade pointed at the dash of the car.

The guard, who for all appearances was fresh out of high school, shone his light on the card inside. "You're Guy Henderson?"

"No. But I'm his mechanic. Well, I was."

"I don't care who you are—you need to leave. Come back tomorrow morning like everyone else." The guard put his hands on his scrawny hips and screwed his mouth up in suspicion.

Elizabeth threw her hands up in the air. "But we weren't—"

"Do I need to call someone to help you find your own car and get in it to drive away?" For emphasis, he tapped at his phone screen.

"No need," Elizabeth said, putting a hand on Kade's arm. "We're going. Thank you."

Elizabeth kept a quick pace, Kade taking big strides to catch up.

"We need to get in that glove box. What are we going to do?"

"Stop assuming it's a single glovebox, for one."

52

"Tell me what you know about Henderson's Classics."

They sat in Kade's truck, halfway up the driveway to Cloud Nine Ranch. He faced the windshield, eyes lost in the distance. He reached for a bag of mints in the center console, offered her one. Elizabeth selected one of the red and white rounds in cellophane wrapping. Kade bit the twisted end of his own mint, unfurling the wrapping.

"There isn't much to know," Kade said, popping the mint in his mouth. He held it between his teeth a moment, then spoke around the disc. "For a reason."

Elizabeth hadn't wanted to wake Rhett at the sound of the big engine. She'd sent Casey a text to let him know they were in the shadowed Ford pulled in at the gate. He'd replied that she shouldn't do anything he wouldn't and sent a winking emoji. *If he only knew we were casing cars the hour before.*

"Let me get this straight. People with lots of disposable income buy cars, fix them up, and then sell them, only to do it all over again."

"You forgot the showing off part, but yeah, that's the gist." Kade sucked on the mint. "Sometimes they get a little more strategic, and it morphs into a full-blown business. As you can imagine, some cars are easier to find, refurbish, and sell. Corvettes and Mustangs, things like that."

"Like Alma's car."

"The Tardis has easy value. It's a classic hot rod the average person would love to own. Not too tough to get parts, in the scheme of things. Easy to turn a profit on the regular."

"But not as lucrative as something more rare." Elizabeth pictured the old Ford.

"It's economics. You can only sell what people are willing to buy. People like Guy make a business out of the low hanging fruit, cars like the Tardis. Then they get a taste for it. Accumulate a specialty collection for the more discriminating tastes. You build a reputation and draw customers with deeper pockets. The older these cars get, the tougher it is to find ones in decent shape. Let alone parts or people willing to machine replacements."

Elizabeth ran a hand across the dash of Kade's truck. Clean, black. An ocean-scented air freshener clung to the air vent, a ballpoint pen in the side door pocket. "How many do you think he sells?"

"When Becky gets me the numbers, I'll know for sure. Best guess is about a dozen a year, at least. And that's just the ones we fix up. Others may just be a straight pass through."

"I thought he was a tech guy."

"He was. Is."

Elizabeth rolled the new information around in her head. Details spiraled outward, like rings radiating from a drop of water on a pond's surface. Guy, a former technology mogul, made a business of buying, fixing up, and selling cars. He had employees manage much of the business but came in person to talk to Raj about an envelope. The same envelope, or one like it, might be in the glove box of one of Guy's cars. The same car he picked up from Raj.

"Can I see the video one more time?"

Kade pulled out his phone and passed it to her. She watched the now familiar scene again. Raj and Guy exchanging pleasantries. Raj reaches behind the counter to bring out the envelope with an invoice on top. The mechanic sliding the stack across the counter, and Guy accepting it. Guy making a comment before picking up the stack.

"Pause!" Elizabeth pointed at the screen, the video stopped. "Look. The envelope isn't opened."

"We call that sealed in my book."

Elizabeth rolled her eyes in the dark.

Kade held up his hands. "Sorry. What am I missing?"

"What if Raj never saw what was in that envelope?"

In the dim dash light, Elizabeth saw Kade's eyebrows knit together. "I don't follow."

"Maybe Guy assumed Raj knew what was inside," Elizabeth said. "Raj could have thought it was the manual or paperwork—something like that—and didn't even look. Why would he? He knew it was Guy's, so he gave it back."

Kade shook his head. "Regardless, why would that matter? That doesn't explain why he broke protocol."

"But that's just it. What if someone didn't try to kill Raj? What if it wasn't about that one envelope, or even Raj?"

"Liz, my best friend was stabbed with a garden fork, and you're telling me it was an accident?"

"I'm saying, what if it was meant to be a warning?"

Kade sat back in the seat, forehead crinkled. "For Raj?"

"For you."

53

"Napkins?"

"Check."

"Bamboo toothpicks?"

"Check."

"Table bunting?"

"I never liked that word. First of all, why is it called bunting? It's not like we have a bunt, or two bunts, and it's not a verb. Second, somehow it sounds cute. Why should hanging fabric be cute?" Casey rifled through a box. He removed a folded piece of fabric and unfurled it. "Check."

Elizabeth stifled a chuckle. Her brother, the designer, was into stylish, trim, and lux. The ruffled, elastic edge of the table wrap violated the bulk of his design preferences. "At least it's black. That screams art opening."

Downtown was busy. People turned out in droves for the day. Casey had parked blocks away. Between them, they hauled equipment and food in Rhett's red wagon. They wove through throngs of people only to resort to alley access.

The gallery occupied the ground floor of a three-story brownstone wedged in along Main Street. The second floor housed an accountant and the third an apartment. According to the historical society, the structure had been a bank, a yarn shop, a massage therapy office, a screenprinter, a toy store, and two different legal firms, a century apart. Its current iteration included a small wine bar and tiny stage saddled to the gallery. The inside was now exposed brick, hardwood floors, and pricing to match. Next to their table, Elizabeth scrutinized a sculpture of what was either two people embracing or alligators engaged in battle. Elizabeth gawked at its four-digit price tag.

Elizabeth and Casey set up next to the stage, tucked into a nook created by the front picture window. They'd arranged the food, tucked kegs behind a table, and given the gallery staff an overview. Elizabeth had insisted they wear all black to distinguish themselves as a classy operation.

"Artsy." Casey plucked a piece of lint from Elizabeth's shoulder. "Black suits you."

"You saying I need to attend more funerals?"

"I'm saying you look like you belong here. I look like a kid who's been wrestled into the hand-me-down Sunday best." Casey tugged at his button-up shirt, the fabric bunched under his arms. "I'm hot. And itchy."

Elizabeth had worried they'd be overdressed, conspicuous. Instead, the crowd had dressed up for the occasion. Exotic fibers draped people dripping with diamonds and too much idle time. "You are right about one thing," she said, after overhearing a woman detailing the stud fees for her stallion to another patron. "These clientele are likely to be right up our alley. Got the cards?"

Casey set a stack of fresh business cards on the table. "Check."

The gallery owner breezed past them with a wave and took to the tiny stage. Manicured nails fiddled with the microphone, then she addressed those gathered. "Welcome, welcome, thank you all for coming. Light refreshments are served to my left. Those of you wishing to purchase can take the number of the piece to the sales counter, and we will be happy to assist."

Sun beat down on the crowd outside, and many ducked into the space to get out of the heat. Besides the invited and monied guests, a steady stream of people wandered in off Main. A few left when they saw the interior of the business. Others continued inside, grateful for the respite, and curious about the art.

Half an hour later, the Blaus were scrambling to keep the table stocked. "How long are we here again?" Elizabeth had changed out a pony keg.

Casey loaded a platter with more sliders. "I told our client up to two hours or until we ran out of food, whichever came first."

"Looks like it might be the latter. People are loving this."

Casey grinned. "You don't think they're here for the art?"

"Haven't seen it yet. They love the brownies, though."

"Go peek in the gallery," Casey said. "If you don't look now, they might sell it all." As he spoke, a couple left with a framed piece wrapped in brown paper.

"If you insist," Elizabeth said, and grinned. She couldn't wait to see the entirety of the work that made for a popular art show in Sheridan.

Elizabeth wandered toward the back of the building and into the exhibit room. On the way, she passed the bulk of gallery art. A smart move on the part of the owner. Remind customers about their regular stock on the way in and out of the building.

Through a brick archway, Elizabeth stepped into a room filled with pictures. Black frames bordered matted photographs. Photos were hung at eye level in groups, with different sizes and subjects.

Elizabeth got closer to the first image on her right, a fender in close-up. Curves and chrome, light and dark. Contrast. The subject filled the frame, drew the eye across the shapes and back. In the next, a photograph of stitching along a back seat had been sewn over with actual thread. In one grouping, the wheel cover was tilted, like Saturn, whitewalls its rings, against a sparkly metallic paint not unlike the night sky. Rounded windows in an old Thunderbird became aquarium glass, the view inside nothing but aquamarine, leather upholstery. She'd never before seen a car as a thing of beauty. A subject to be captured. Admired. Now, she studied the pieces, their shapes and the light. This person was good. Real good.

"Enjoying the show?"

"Very much," Elizabeth said.

Kade stood at her side. He held his hands behind his back in parade rest. Both of them regarded a smaller photograph.

"You like this one?"

Elizabeth nodded. "I do. I think it's my favorite."

"Why is that?"

The image was a closeup of a disco ball, hung from a dash. In each of the tiny mirrors, parts of the car's interior were copied: steering wheel, head rests, shifter, and door handles. Vehicle, deconstructed. "It's as if you're seeing the sum of a thousand parts."

"Took me a hundred shots to get it right," Kade said.

"You...are the artist?" Elizabeth's breath caught in her throat.

Kade smiled. "I am. Boy was I glad when you found her keychain," he continued. "Alma loaned me the darn thing for a weekend, and I lost it. Don't know where you found it, but it saved my bacon."

Elizabeth was stunned. The keychain must have fallen out of Kade's pocket when he climbed onto the stage to help Thor.

She turned to take in the room, in the entirety of this work on display. Photograph after photograph. "This is all...you?" It was a statement shaded in a question.

Kade nodded. “We aren’t always as slammed down at the shop. Have to keep myself busy in the downtimes.”

“This is all so...incredible.” She admired a wall-sized print of a row of cars, each shinier than the next, a rainbow of metal.

“Thank you,” he said, and shrugged. “That means a lot to me.

Elizabeth shook her head. “I’ll be right back. I’m going to murder my brother.”

“For?”

“Yet again failing to disclose our client.”

54

Jo handed over one backpack, a half-empty bag of kettle corn, and two little boys. "I fed them hot dogs, too, so they should be full for a half hour at least. Though Rhett ate more ketchup than anything else."

"Sounds about right," Elizabeth said. "Thanks for bringing them."

"Happy to," Jo said. "I wanted to check out the cars. Clint is always threatening to disappear into the garage after retirement. If that's what he's going to do, I want to make sure his mistress is something I want to drive when it's finished."

"And which of these beauties would that be?" The women looked out across the sea of cars. Double the number present the night before, they stretched on for blocks. Everything from the first decade of automobiles to a souped-up truck was on display. There were even a few specialty entries that year, including a DeLorean, its doors open like wings. In half a block of reading informational placards for each vehicle, Elizabeth's knowledge of car history had tripled.

"How is the art show?"

"You mean the part where Casey avoided telling me it was for Kade—again?" Elizabeth sighed. "It was actually pretty great. Casey booked a few more events. We gave out all our cards as well as the food. Had to close up shop early as we ran out."

"That's wonderful," Jo said. "About the gig. And Kade."

"Don't you dare start taking Casey's side on this," Elizabeth said.

The boys stopped to watch a man manipulate two giant sticks and string to blow giant bubbles into the air. Massive blobs floated up and over the cars. Some cleared rooftops before the inevitable pop.

"I'll re-examine my liaisons," Jo said, "if you admit to me that you and Kade are more than friends.

"We have absolutely not gone past first base if that's what you are asking."

"Since when is that an indicator of anything these days? Though in my ancient opinion, it still should be, but that's a story for another day. My mother set each of us down, my brothers and sisters alike. She insisted that we wouldn't be able to expect anyone to buy a cow if we gave away the milk for free. That was the closest she came to a talk about the birds and the bees, but we got the message."

"Look," Elizabeth said. "I do appreciate a good animal husbandry metaphor, but I'm not sure I'm ready to claim anything specific yet. We've talked, but..."

"Let me guess. It's complicated?"

The women continued walking with the crowd, the boys holding hands between them.

"I've got a track record of letting men walk all over me, and I've just come up for air from that. I'm not exactly itching to dive back down into the depths of being a doormat."

"I'd like to see you trust yourself enough to choose a man who wouldn't do that to you."

"You and me, both," Elizabeth said. They passed a trio of vendors: sunglasses, hats, and bandanas. People flocked to the tents to get sun protection. A mother squatted down to place strawberry-shaped shades on her child and refill a water bottle. "I'm not sure where

Kade's at right now. He's slammed at work and I'm not sure he has the headspace for a relationship—yet. Not with what happened to Raj."

"Speaking of that. Remember how the handle of the trident was covered in fingerprints?"

"Thor's prints were there, too. Think back to his costume," Jo said

Elizabeth could see Thor in her mind. Body splayed across the stage, emergency personnel surrounding him. She thought of Thor at the party, alive and well.

"Yeah? Toga, that sparkly belt thing. Big hammer. Fairly Hollywood."

"And *gloves*," Jo said.

55

A faint buzzing came from over Elizabeth's head, and she gave the air an absent-minded swat. When the sound continued, she looked up. Above her, a drone, a dozen feet in the air, traced the sidewalk. Then it crossed the street and dipped into an alley. She returned her attention to Jo. "How did Clint learn this?"

"Social media, where one learns everything these days."

"But if he was involved..." Elizabeth remembered the rush to the stage. The broken trombone. "Did they figure out how he died?"

"Anaphylaxis. Peanut allergy."

"But where...how?"

Jo shrugged. "That part's still under investigation." They stopped at a snow cone vendor, and she bought the boys cups of mounded ice. Swirls of color indicated the exact shade of tongue each boy would earn. Purple for Rhett, green for Benny.

Elizabeth purchased a soft pretzel, dusted with salty bits, and tore off a chunk. The soft dough gave her something to chew on while she considered the news. *Had Thor removed his gloves to stab Raj? Why would someone allergic to nuts die playing at a band concert?*

With Main Street closed to traffic, they strolled its center, stopping at one car and then another. The boys' eyes lit up at the vintage fire truck. Benny was all smiles when a fireman lifted him into the seat so Jo could snap a picture.

"How's brewing?" The fireman flashed Elizabeth a toothy grin. He'd been a worthy competitor in the home brewer's contest.

"Not too bad. I've got an orange wheat on. Still figuring out my hazy."

"You should come out to my place sometime. I'd love to get your thoughts on a few I've got on tap. We could bounce ideas off each other over a pint...or two. And dinner."

Oh. Elizabeth glanced at his left hand. Bare. He could be one of those who didn't wear a ring, or he could be single. Still. "I'm working on some brews at the moment," she said, by way of a hint. "But thank you."

With a nod, he moved on to greet the next person. She collected Benny and rejoined their group.

"I'm pretty sure he hit on me," Elizabeth whispered.

"And?"

Elizabeth shot Jo a look. "And I'm already taken. I think."

Jo lifted an eyebrow. "Taken or not, most women would take that kind of interaction as a compliment. As long as he wasn't creepy."

"Not creepy. All right, I am flattered." They continued walking.

Next to a classic VW Beetle, Alma occupied a green and pink striped lawn chair next to the Tardis. She beamed at the onlookers.

"Well, don't you look pleased as punch," Jo said. "Glad you came?"

"No. My face aches from all this smiling and chit chat." Alma pushed and prodded at her cheeks.

"I may be an amateur at car shows," Elizabeth said, "but aren't you supposed to talk to everyone about your car?"

"Well yeah, or so I thought. Most want to talk about their own cars, not mine. But it is fun to be a woman who knows a lot about cars.

I'm earning some serious street cred. I've even had a few offers on the Tardis."

"You aren't selling, are you?" Elizabeth reached out to the pearlescent paint on the trunk. The metal was hot, and she retracted her fingers.

"No way. Dad would murder me. But it means I am doing things right. And I've been able to generate business for the shop." She pointed to a sign perched on the hood of the car. The Kade's Garage logo was printed on the cardstock. "I figure it can't hurt."

Elizabeth spotted a small tablet in Alma's hands. The woman consulted the screen and tapped at the controls. "What are you looking at?"

"I got a new drone for camera work," she said. "I wanted to get some overhead shots of the car show to use in our promotions."

"Oh, so that was you flying by a minute ago?"

Alma shook her head. "No way. I'm staying away from people. Got most of my vehicle footage before the crowd got here. I'd love to get some with the streets packed, but I'm not willing to risk that yet."

"They regulate all that," Jo said. "Makes it easy when Clint has to step in. Most people don't bother with licensing and registration."

"It's a big skill on a set, so I took the course, got my papers. Anyone in the film industry should," Alma said. She held up the app console. "I'm checking my battery stats. I want to do an aerial of my car and a few others, but I need to wait for a recharge and a break in the crowds."

"Looking to expand your own restoration business?"

"I'm not making the kind of cash where I can get into that hobby. A feature length film or two away from that, likely. Not him though." She nudged her chin.

Elizabeth followed the gesture and spotted the Ford 40. The man from the news, linen blazer, tan lines, and a smile that didn't reach his eyes, chatted with another man next to the open hood. Guy rested a palm on the hood of the car, a proud owner. His expensive watch flashed in the light. Closer, and in person, Elizabeth figured him to be pushing sixty. A smudge of brown at his collar hinted at a tinted moisturizer if not foundation. Here was a man who wanted—no, *needed*—to look good.

The women watched as Guy shook hands with the man, who reached for his wallet. Guy put a hand on the man's arm and handed over a key ring. He reached in through the driver's side window and removed the For Sale sign, tearing it into pieces. Guy pointed toward the north end of the street, talking. The man nodded. With a clap on the back from Guy, the other man got into the car and backed out, slow and steady. The crowd parted around him like the river around a canoe. Guy saluted the driver.

When he turned back toward the sidewalk, Elizabeth caught his eye. She flushed and looked away. *Act casual, Liz.* She shaded her eyes with one hand and pretended to be searching across the event.

"Looks like it sold," Alma said. "I'll text Kade."

"Don't you usually sign paperwork or something?" Elizabeth squinted in the direction of the departed car. She thought of the envelope possibly inside.

Alma shrugged. "They've got a spillover spot down at the end. Tables with a notary and everything. People buy and sell here like crazy. Paperwork is handled down there."

Elizabeth wondered if the day's receipts would be tallied, a known figure. Guy's actions made the exchange appear to be a done deal. She started to suggest they take the boys to see the classic tractor when an announcement over big speakers drew their attention to the stage.

Guy waited behind the microphone for the crowd to quiet. He had his hands together, the posture of a giver.

Silence settled, and he opened his address. "You may have seen a few of my toys out here." Those gathered who knew him tittered at the humble brag. Others knew that, at the least, this man likely owned a car or two. He continued. "But I brought something new with me today, something without wheels. And it's going to change how we do business."

56

Guy moved his hand through the air, as though waving people in for supper. On cue, a pair of drones cruised down the street, toward the stage. They flew well above the heads of the crowd.

"Clint is going to hate this," Jo whispered to Elizabeth. "Hope he got a permit. Not that he can't afford a fine."

The boys stared in awe at the drones as Guy continued to speak.

"How many of you have ever chased down a car over the internet only to roll up at some dilapidated barn and discover the floorboard rusted out, with half the engine in the dirt?"

Hands raised above the crowd. Guy continued. "You have to start your search all over again. Not to mention the time and mileage you spent. I have a solution that will change the way we shop for our restoration projects."

The drones zipped back to the stage. Necks craned to watch their flight. Each drone had a blue belly and a silver top. On approach, they executed a neat flip in mid-air and landed with a soft click on Guy's left and right.

Giant screens on either side of the stage displayed the view from each drone's camera. People jostled those around them to get a closer look at the machines. With a sweep of his hand, Guy sent them back into the sky.

The pair buzzed each other in a figure-eight, then each approached a car on opposite sides of the street. Elizabeth recognized these as other cars Kade had identified.

"As you see," Guy said, commandeering attention back to the stage, "we'll do the hard work for you." He pointed to the screens behind him.

On the left screen, the camera panned the length of one car. On the right, the view was of the undercarriage of the other car. Elizabeth looked back at the vehicles themselves. The drones cased the outsides, filming the entire time. They carved a path around each car, becoming intimate with every inch of exposed surface. One drone went to work capturing images of the engine, a slow pan to give the viewer time to assess.

"I introduce Air Concierge. This service is designed for the discriminating collector. No longer will you have to drive out to some tiny map dot to learn if the promised Phaeton is a gem or a dud. Drones will be the first line of inquiry. They will capture the asset's current state and display it for you in real time. You won't have to question your investment or risk being outbid by someone nearby. My pilots are on call, 24/7." Murmurs filtered through the crowd. Guy continued, "We can do more than cars. Boats, farming equipment, the farms themselves. Heck, we could check out a herd of cattle if that's what you want. I employ FAA drone pilots who know how to get the visuals you need for your business."

"Sounds like an Uber for used car sales," Jo said to Elizabeth. "There are worse ideas. I took a bus down to Casper once to pick up a Subaru described as in mint condition. I got there, and the thing had lawn chairs for seats and no trunk."

Elizabeth pictured her own car under drone scrutiny. "Guess you passed on that one?"

"Let's just say it was more like an El Camino, minus intention."

Whispers turned into chatter as those gathered discussed the drones. The pilots remained hidden from sight. Elizabeth peered up at the second story windows in the old brick buildings. *What kind of range do they need?*

Rhett and Benny hadn't taken their eyes off the drones, nor had most in the crowd. Elizabeth stared after the machines and frowned. The premise made sense, especially in a big state where many people lived far away from others. Something about the business model tugged at her thoughts. How often would people need a drone preview?

At this, Elizabeth gasped, a soft inhalation.

"Subscribers will have access to our exclusive app in which you can order service, store footage, and communicate with buyers and sellers. We can do a la carte runs for single purchases, too. If you like what you see, we can even handle the purchase for you. I have guys—and ladies—at the ready to ship assets to you. Air Concierge is a one stop shop as we take care of every detail. For more demonstrations, stop by my booth. At Air Concierge, we want to be your eyes in the sky." At this, Guy pointed down Main, and the drones zoomed off, disappearing into the sunshine.

The crowd cheered. Guy passed the microphone to the next speaker and took the short flight of steps off the stage. He was crushed by a gaggle of eager customers. Guy shook hands with many and started walking. People followed, clamoring for a chance to talk with him about what they'd seen.

"Jo, can you watch the kids? I have to find Kade. Or Clint. Now."

57

Before Jo could question or object, Elizabeth took off down the sidewalk. She slipped between couples, danced around strollers, and hopped over an idle dog. People crowded the sidewalks. They stopped to look at cars, talk to neighbors, and peer into shop windows. She did her best to tamp down frustration at the pace and keep moving forward.

At Brundage, Elizabeth turned to aim for the alley and ran. Brick wall after brick wall corralled her vision as she headed for the far end of the event. Her sneakers pounded the pavement, a rhythmic slap that echoed between the buildings. She had to get to Kade, tell him what she knew.

The art show was a success, people streamed in and out of the little gallery all morning. Kade had said he'd stay away from the madness of the cars. With the gallery in the morning and cars occupying the rest of his day, he'd closed the shop. He'd told her there was no point in staying open with everyone downtown, and to market, you need to be where the people are. Thanks to Alma, Elizabeth knew to run north.

Keep breathing, Liz. Her heart thudded in her chest as her lungs burned through oxygen. Her shins screamed from the hard surface, but she kept going.

At each cross street, she turned her head to check her relationship to the event. The first block hosted the food carts, her favorite barbecue spot at the center. Next came more cars, between which a clown on stilts made balloon animals for kids. Block by block, she willed herself onward.

Kade was likely safe and sound, nestled among the other business owners. He was likely deep in car talk with others, debating the latest paint colors or polymers. Elizabeth would find him, talk to him, and they would figure out what to do next. Together. He shouldn't be alone.

Elizabeth checked the next street. Vintage cars lined this street, too, but with fewer admirers. *This must be the holding spot Alma mentioned.* Two men haggled over the price of a Corsair, one holding his hand over the mic end of a phone. Beyond them, the booths. She saw a banner for Kade's Garage zip-tied across the front of one spot next to another for a tire center. She could see Kade in his work shirt, hair slicked back underneath a trucker hat. He stood with his arms crossed, one hand on his chin. A woman in a wide straw hat beamed at him, and Elizabeth froze in her tracks.

The woman said something that made Kade laugh. He reached across the table to fetch something, and the woman took in the view of his backside. He turned back to hand her his card, and she smiled, bright and innocent. A flicker of jealousy pitted in Elizabeth's stomach.

Thirty more feet and she'd be there, with him. She pictured herself, in his arms, resting against his chest. This woman would go away, dismissed, and she, the girlfriend, would tell him everything.

Elizabeth had been so foolish to keep her distance from this man. He'd held a torch for her so long it had started to burn his fingers. She knew that now. Knew that life was short, and when you found good people, you needed to hold onto them, keep them close. She kicked herself for the time she wasted without him.

Overhead, a drone hovered. Its propellers whirred, and sunlight glinted off its shiny top. The drone dipped and buzzed around the back of Kade's booth.

Elizabeth started to shout a warning. A gloved hand clamped around her mouth, silencing her. Her eyes went wide as she was dragged backward. She stumbled to regain her footing. Her hands flailed in the air, wild. She struggled against her captor, but fumes from the gloves made her head swim. The hand was replaced with a gag as she was pulled into the alley. She tried to twist out from under the grip, but her captor wrenched hard on her neck. Elizabeth winced from pain and her knees buckled. She hit the pavement hard and gave a muffled shriek into the rag stuffed in her mouth.

The attacker flipped Elizabeth onto her stomach and tied her hands together. They blindfolded her, then knelt to her ear, a knee in her back. "Want this to be over?" The voice was stern, a hoarse whisper, but falsified.

Elizabeth yelled against the gag but another pop to her vertebrae and she melted onto the pavement. She tried to nod but pain rocketed up her spine. She gritted her teeth at the sharp protest in her neck.

"Then stop fighting me."

Dizzy and disoriented, tears ran down her cheeks. Kade was steps away, and she hadn't been able to call for him. What were they going to do with her?

Elizabeth's last thought was of her son, playing in a field of poppies.

58

The world glowed red, or so it seemed.

Elizabeth's consciousness swam into recognition. What appeared at first to be the inside of her eyelid was instead a red bandanna tied over her eyes. She was cramped in a tight space, bent into the fetal position. Her head ached as did her wrists under their restraints. She felt around with her fingers and determined her hands were bound with a zip-tie. Her bound ankles suggested similar treatment.

As Elizabeth wriggled, her cheek brushed against the surface of her containment. The scratchy material was a carpet, of sorts. She attempted to stretch her limbs, only to find the walls of the space within inches of her extremities. It was then she heard the hum of an engine, its rattling a soft vibration underneath her. The scent of leather, polish, and lemons lingered in the air, as though the carpet had been freshly shampooed. On impulse, Elizabeth lifted her head.

Thunk. She knocked against metal. Realization rushed to her gut. She was stuck in the trunk of a car.

Think, she told herself, willing the pretzel to stay in her stomach. *Don't panic, Liz. Think.*

Whether from fear or the restraints, blood pounded in Elizabeth's head. Her mouth was dry from the gag, and her fingers had gone numb, their tips ghosts at the end of her hands. She rotated her lower shoulder to reposition her elbow. The pressure lessened. As blood rushed back into her hands, she counted down from ten in her mind. Far from abated, her panic did ease a half beat, long enough for her to focus.

Elizabeth wished herself anywhere but there, anytime but then. The car idled along with her options. Its engine rumbled, like a sleepy giant waking up. Whomever had stuffed her in here was more than likely in the driver's seat, a few feet away.

Elizabeth shifted again so her hands could move. Feeling returned to her fingertips. Her only directional information came from the sound of the motor. Careful movement gave her brief access to the back of the space. She found a seam in the rear of the car. Through the small gap came the heat of the afternoon. Crimped metal formed an edge. An exit.

Jumbled voices outside. Muted discussion. An angry shout.

With her feet, Elizabeth toed the space where her fingertips couldn't reach. With the toe of her shoe, she traced the edging as far as her ankle would twist. Then, she inched her fingers across the surface again. A new vinyl stretched across the metal exterior. *An upgrade.*

The rumble seat. *Raj.*

Elizabeth pressed her face to the carpet to inch the blindfold up her forehead. Sharp pain shot through her neck, a reminder of her attacker. She squeezed her eyes shut, then opened them again. Slowly, she rotated her head to look around. Through the gap, she could see the interior of the space.

Cream-colored fabric, cherry red paint. The Ford Model 40.

Elizabeth remembered her conversation with Raj. Recalled his words as he detailed the challenges of custom restorations. *No locks. Couldn't find replacements in time.*

She'd found a kernel of hope. *But where am I? What if they're outside?*

Then she thought of Rhett. Casey. Jo and Clint. Marg. Kade. All the people who meant more to her than anything. She chose bravery.

After a quick prayer, Elizabeth scrunched her knees all the way to her chest. In one swift motion, she gave a solid kick to the back of the car. To her surprise, the back popped open, and sunlight burst in.

59

Elizabeth sat up, one eye blinking into the light. Her blindfold hung half across her face. The scene around her came into focus.

Next to the car stood a woman on the sidewalk. Her mouth was frozen in a wide O. She stared straight at Elizabeth as shock kept her rooted.

A second passed, and Elizabeth realized that the woman was screaming. The sound flooded in all at once. Behind it came a rush of footsteps.

"Get her out of there!"

"Whose car is that?"

"Call the police! Call someone!"

"Get out of my way!"

Elizabeth recognized the last voice. Kade.

Hands removed the blindfold from Elizabeth's head, then moved to the knot at the back of her neck. In a moment, the fabric was whipped from her mouth. She coughed and spluttered, then gasped for air. Her teeth were gritty.

"Get her water! We need water!"

Gentle arms scooped up her body and set her on the sidewalk. She smelled orange and pine. Kade.

Kade didn't let go. He held her upright, stable. Elizabeth's breath heaved.

From above her, a bottle of water appeared. Kade grabbed it, twisted off the cap, and held it to her lips.

"I've got a knife. I'll get the ties." This was Alma's voice.

First Elizabeth's wrists and then her ankles were freed. Her body sagged, released from the bindings. She didn't trust herself to move much. The edges of her vision were blurry. To negotiate standing up, let alone walking, seemed an impossible concept.

"She was in the rumble seat," Kade said, anger a sharp hum at the edges of his voice.

"Of the 40?" Alma, incredulous.

Elizabeth sipped at the water offered to her. When she paused to look around, she saw the Tardis, parked perpendicular to the Ford. Sirens wailed in the distance. She croaked, "How did you know where I was?"

"I didn't," Kade said. His eyes searched hers, desperate. She saw in them raw pools of worry. "That was all Alma."

Alma stepped forward to block the sun that beamed down on their gathering. The filmmaker-turned-mechanic lifted her shoulders in a muted shrug and pointed at the tiny machine abandoned on the sidewalk. "When I saw you take off running, I followed you. From the air."

The drone. What Elizabeth had seen, why she'd been after Kade, came back to her in an instant. "I have to talk to Clint," she rasped. "I have to tell him who was after Raj."

Alma exchanged a look with Kade, who gave her a brief nod. She handed Elizabeth an ice pack. "Don't worry, I already did."

60

A cool washcloth pressed against Elizabeth's forehead. Rivulets of water squished out and dripped down her face.

Casey crouched over his sister. "You look like a drowned rat."

Elizabeth was tucked under the crisp, white hospital sheets of a room in Sheridan Memorial. She'd recanted her story for her brother, both to share and to remember the details. Sheriff Wolf called to assure her Rhett was safe and away from the crowd. He would be by to take her statement shortly.

Casey listened as Elizabeth traced her route from Jo and the kids, through the alley, and the attack. Someone had been after her. Purposeful. Her head pounded from the attempt to rationalize the events of the afternoon.

"I feel like one," Elizabeth said. The IV at her side dripped, a steady reminder she was hooked up. A victim of a crime she'd yet to wrap her head around.

"I'm here to listen if there's more to share, but there's a swarthy mechanic itching to see you. As I'm your closest kin, so they wouldn't let him in without my say-so, given the circumstances."

"Should I put on a little lipstick?" Elizabeth gave Casey a weak smile.

Casey tilted his head and considered her. He wrinkled his nose. "I don't think it would help."

Elizabeth socked him, a playful punch. The movement made her wince, a glaring reminder of the bruises around her wrists.

He rubbed at his forearm in mock pain. "I was going to say that he doesn't seem the type to care about that. Sheesh."

Elizabeth reached out again to squeeze his arm. "Thanks, brother."

Casey kissed her on the forehead. He hadn't done that since the night before he left their parents' house, never to return. Casey had read her a chapter from Tolkien and tucked her into bed. Her last childhood memory of him was his back, heading out the door.

Like today, like now. This time, though, as he disappeared from her sight, she knew he would wait outside her door. Knew he was a permanent fixture in her life. Someone who wasn't going anywhere until the end.

This realization had been a process. A proof of concept made possible through night after night of his not leaving. Of their family game nights, Sunday Suppers, and afternoons in the barn. It was the way he interacted with Rhett, made him a priority. His nephew, his buddy. This came from thousands of moments threaded together with new meaning to a blood relationship turned family tie. It had taken months, but security settled over her like an invisible blanket upon the bed. A little ragged on corners and patched in places, but it was comforting, and it was hers.

In seconds, there was a soft tap on the door. "Knock, knock?"

"Please come in," Elizabeth said. When Kade peeked around the door, she continued. "As you can see, I've set out my finest tea service." She waved a hand at the half-empty cups of cold hospital coffee and a muffin encased in plastic wrapping.

"And here I am without a tie. May I still join you?" Kade lifted his eyebrows.

"Yes," Elizabeth said, a simple request. "Please."

Kade crossed the room. From behind his back, he withdrew an offering and held it out to her. He cradled a small bouquet of daisies and miniature roses, nestled in a bright blue coffee mug.

"Congratulations, it's a boy," Elizabeth read from the ceramic surface.

"It was that or the black mug that said Sorry for Your Loss. Which seemed problematic in a different way. I almost had to wrestle a sweet old lady for this one."

Elizabeth grimaced. "She would have cleaned your clock. My gran was feisty."

"No doubt," Kade said. "She settled on a teddy bear instead."

"Whew." Elizabeth held the mug in her hands. Baby's breath flowers peppered the arrangement, tiny and delicate. How long had it been since someone gave her something, a token? Not someone. A person who meant more and more to her every day. First one tear and then another slid down her cheeks to fall in wet dots on the cheap fabric covering the bed.

Kade waited, quiet. He reached out a hand to hold hers. "You scared me there."

Elizabeth licked at her lip. Her tongue traced a crack, split and scabbed over. "I was running to you."

Kade shook his head. "You don't have to run anymore."

61

Sheriff Wolf filled the doorframe of Elizabeth's hospital room. He removed his glasses, polished the lenses with a cloth from his pocket, and put them back across his nose. "You look different," he said.

"Road rash will do that for a girl. Natural dermabrasion."

Wolf nodded, respectful. "This isn't a social call, but I'll pass that advice on to the missus. Jo's been griping at her mirror."

"Am I under arrest?" Elizabeth cracked jokes to help pretend she didn't have the shakes. Couldn't still feel the rough carpet of the Ford's interior on her cheeks. "If you're here to get my adrenaline going again, it'll be another hour before they release me. If I had a dollar for every time that nurse comes in here to check my blood pressure..."

The sheriff held a folder in his hands. He extracted several large photographs and showed them to Elizabeth. "These are from Alma's drone camera. She said if I didn't show them to you now, she would during visitor's hours.

Elizabeth flipped through the images. Blown up, the pictures were a little fuzzy, blurred. The drone must have been following her from a few dozen feet away. There she was, running down the alley. Another snap from right before she spotted Kade. In this one, a figure appeared behind her in the frame, a step behind. She flipped back to the prior photograph and saw the Ford parked in the alley.

She returned to the other photo and squinted at the person. Ball cap, jeans. A ponytail.

"No face shot?"

"Alma's battery died at the worst moment. What she saw was enough to get us over there, thank God."

Elizabeth screwed up her face. "I thought that guy bought the Ford." She thought of the squat man in the Hawaiian shirt. He couldn't have chased her down—and why would he? "I don't understand."

"Do either of you recognize the person in these images at all?"

Black and white and blurred was all Elizabeth saw. "I don't. I'm sorry."

"That's a hat from the shop," Kade said. "I gave away a couple dozen at the show to potential clients, so I can't be sure."

Elizabeth thought of the woman in the straw hat who'd fawned over Kade. She frowned and brought the picture closer to her face. "Could it be an employee? But you only have a few left."

"One of them was the camera person," Clint said.

"And one is here," Kade said.

Elizabeth sat up, her body protesting. "Raj is here?"

62

Kade pushed Elizabeth down the corridor in a wheelchair. She read each room number they passed to quell her building anxiety.

"Why didn't you tell me?"

From behind her, Kade's voice was measured. Careful. "He wanted to keep it quiet."

"I don't understand."

The squeak of the wheels against the linoleum echoed off the walls. Nurses in a rainbow of scrubs brushed past them. A few eyed Elizabeth's wristband and then her escort.

"I'm not the type to tell another person's story," Kade said. "Not when they can tell you themselves."

A security guard leaned on the counter at the nurse's station, chatting up an attendant. He gave Kade a curt nod and returned to the conversation.

"That was a look," Elizabeth whispered, her voice still hoarse at its edges.

"Let's say that people are a bit on edge after what happened. Especially when it could all be related."

Elizabeth had more questions, but Kade had backed up to the door of a room. He pushed it open with his hip and pulled her inside.

They entered a room with two beds. In the first, a man aimed a remote at a television screen. He flicked through channels rapid-fire. The curtain was drawn between him and the person by the window.

Raj.

Kade wheeled Elizabeth forward. Behind the edge of the curtain, Raj was tucked into his own bed. He stared out the window, faint sunbeams on his cheeks. When he heard the visitors, he turned their way. "Hey," he said, a soft greeting.

"Hi," Elizabeth said. Sudden shyness washed over her like a spring rain. She mumbled apologies. "I'm sorry. I didn't know…I would have visited…smuggled Leia in at least. Why are you here alone? I didn't think you were here this whole time, recovering. Wouldn't you rather be home?"

The smile on Raj's face faltered for a moment, a fine crack in stability. "I…I told Kade I didn't want any visitors. And, well…I can't really go home."

"Why? I've seen pictures of you, from the paper. All you've done for the community. And Kade called your mom. I bet they'd love to have you back."

Raj met her eyes. "I'd love to be there. But…" He trailed off.

"Either of you want something from the vending machines?" Kade hooked a thumb over his shoulder. "I'm craving one of those overpriced bags of jerky right about now. Eh?"

Elizabeth shook her head. Raj did the same. Kade saluted them and backed out the door.

"Subtle," Elizabeth said.

"He's a good friend," Raj said. He shifted in his bed. With the press of a button, he raised the back a little higher. "Too good, really."

"I'm learning that," Elizabeth said. "He's said the same about you, by the way."

Raj squeezed his eyes shut for a brief moment. "Kade was good to me when I'd burned about every bridge I had. Gave me a lifeline. A fresh start. I owe him so much."

The second hand on the wall clock ticked, rhythmic. Outside the window, a squirrel skittered up a cottonwood. "I saw the articles. You've done more than a little good yourself. Young Mechanics Club. That eco car team. How you manage to do all that from several states away, I can only imagine. I can barely keep my life together in one place."

Raj was quiet, thinking. He sighed and looked up. "I can't go home."

Elizabeth tried not to stare at the bulky midline of Raj's body. *Bandages.* The grim reality of what he'd suffered was front and center. "Can't?"

The mechanic lifted his shoulders and released them in a shrug of acceptance. "I got into trouble as a kid. Big trouble. The kind where the cops get involved. They let teenage me free in exchange for names. I handed them over."

Elizabeth appraised Raj. He didn't seem the type to break the law. "How bad were you?"

"Drugs, bad. Stolen cars, bad."

"Oh."

Raj held one hand in the other, mashed a palm with the opposite thumb. "Got mixed up with certain groups. Spent two months locked up. It was suggested that if I didn't want to end up back in juvie, I needed to get far, far away. Somewhere I wouldn't be tempted. Would be hard to find." Raj's face crumpled with the memories.

Elizabeth gestured to the window. Outside the glass, beyond the tree, was a stretch of mown grass. An older couple perched on a nearby bench, a Yorkie in the woman's lap. Next to the man was a rolled up newspaper and a bouquet of lilies. "You did come to the middle of nowhere. From the most populated state to the least."

"I thought I had. Until I make a mistake—and the past—came back to haunt me."

"The envelope?"

Raj nodded. "I should have handed it over to the Boss Man. Seemed get excited over an envelope when I could just give it back. Didn't even think to look inside. It's obvious now that Guy didn't take my word on that."

"Is that why there's a man with a gun outside that door, doing his best to land a date with the desk clerk?"

"That's my guess, though I haven't been told much. Wolf said there's an ongoing investigation. Had me make a statement, then came back later with more questions."

Elizabeth knew the frustration of wanting answers. "I have a confession," Elizabeth started. "You know how they say 62% of people are on the internet?"

"I didn't, but go on."

Elizabeth looked down at her hands. "I may have googled you. A little."

Raj's eyebrows went up. His cheeks were sunken, his skin dulled. *Hospital food,* Elizabeth thought. She wondered how long he had left to heal from the extent of his injuries.

"Unexpected," Raj concluded. "But maybe...flattering?"

"I was trying to figure out who attacked you. I worried they'd come after Kade."

"And?"

Elizabeth wrung her hands, unsure of where to start. She opened her mouth to explain when Kade returned, a package under one arm, his hands full of snack bags.

"I found jerky. I've also got a Fast Break, two bags of Doritos, some of that trail mix with the chocolate pieces, and a pack of fruity gum. Not exactly the food pyramid but I had to work with what was there."

"Perfect timing," Raj said. "Your girlfriend was about to explain why she cyberstalked me."

Kade cocked an eyebrow, then flopped into the visitor's chair. He crossed an ankle over the opposite knee and tore into a bag of chips. "Go on. This ought to be good."

Elizabeth rolled her eyes. "Thanks for the support." She turned back to Raj. "I found out about your charity work. For someone who never goes home, you sure send a lot of money in your place."

Raj's cheeks reddened, and he chewed on his lip. "I want kids like me, or the me I was back then, to have a shot. A chance at a real life. That's all."

"Becky told me about your automatic deductions to a California bank. She found them when she verified payroll," Kade said.

Elizabeth scowled. Why did that woman's name get brought up in every aspect of Kade's business? Would a relationship with Kade have to include one with Becky?

Raj had similar feelings. "Why do you keep her around? You know she's bad news."

"Not this again. She's good at what she does. Saved me thousands in streamlining supply orders. We were ordering three different kinds of gloves. Three! She's saved me her salary and then some in all the errors she's found. That woman has an eye for business. Besides, Boyd left her with a barn full of horses and drained accounts. She needs the work until she can get on her feet."

The mention of tight finances stung with familiarity for Elizabeth. If Kade knew about her situation, would she receive the same pitying commentary? Elizabeth worried over that possibility.

Raj scoffed. "Sure, she claims to be taking classes at the college. I'd bet it's a scam to get her claws into you."

"Enough about business. You're still on leave, and there's probably some law about that. But, I brought you something. From the car club."

Kade reached for the wrapped item he'd carried in and gave it to Raj.

"What's this?" Raj didn't wait for Kade's answer. He hooked a thumb under a piece of tape affixed to automotive advertisements. "Glad to see you're recycling."

"We aren't exactly stocked up on fancy wrapping at the shop," Kade said.

As the paper fell away, Raj held a small plaque in his hands. His lips moved as he read it. Finished, tears welled at the corners of his eyes. "You did this, for me?"

"This was all you."

"Can I see?"

Raj held out the plaque to Elizabeth. When she took it, he wiped at his face with the back of one hand while she read it aloud. "*In commemoration of his outstanding contributions to the automotive industry, we hereby establish the Raj Singh Young Mechanics Scholarship for students at Sheridan College.*" She turned to Kade. "What does that mean?"

Kade clasped his hands around his knees. "It means that the club wants to help keep the apprentice program going. And in Raj's name."

Raj withdrew a tissue from a box on the bedside stand and wiped at his eyes. "I don't know what to say."

"I also got a hold of Pranjali. Let her know how you're doing."

"You called my mom?"

"I needed to ask her to help get me in touch with the coach for the car team. How am I supposed to know where you went to high school? At any rate, Kade's Garage will sponsor them every year I'm in business. With luck, we can establish a sister team here."

Raj's lip quivered. "I don't understand. I'm just a mechanic. I didn't think...I didn't know..." He shook his head in disbelief.

Kade reached out to give the bed a brief pat. "This world is made better through true leadership. Not those blowhards who throw money at problems that don't exist only to buy themselves a yacht in appreciation of their own good work."

Guy. The business owner was a crab in a bucket, stepping on others in a quest to get out. In contrast, Kade and Raj reached out to others, lifting them up.

Kade continued. "People who know what it's like for things to be tough are the ones we need out there, making a difference. Those who want to make it easier for the next person. I'm proud that you're an employee but even more proud to call you my friend. We need a million more like you."

And like you, Kade, Elizabeth thought. *People who look for the good in others and find ways to show the world that goodness.*

Raj covered his mouth with one hand, as though to hold back another round of tears. After a moment, he said, "Thank you."

63

"You know," she said, "I want to try to walk."

Elizabeth's body ached in new places, but she was able to shift herself to the edge of the bed. Like Raj, she'd used the remote to turn the bed into a chaise lounge, her perch on which to await imminent freedom.

"You could try," Kade said. "But sometimes we should let others take care of us so we can heal."

"I do need to get better at that," Elizabeth said.

Kade put a hand to his chest. "From one independent person to another, I can empathize. It's easy for me to preach, it's another to walk the talk. I admit to being in protective mode, but I can back off."

Elizabeth considered this man, this moment. "How about a little longer? I am still in a hospital."

A nurse pressed into the room. Behind him, Casey followed.

"I'm here to spring you," her brother said. He nodded at the nurse who'd begun an assessment of Elizabeth's vitals. "Assuming you pass this here professional's assessment."

"What's the word out there?" Kade's tone was serious, in stark contrast to her brother's light-hearted entrance.

Casey pushed the curtains aside and looked out into the courtyard. He pressed against the window ledge, kicking one ankle over the other. "Good news or bad news first?"

"Bad news," Elizabeth and Kade chimed together.

"There was an envelope in the glove box of the Ford. Why would a car for sale come stuffed with cash? The guy with the key tried to say he was just test driving. He's still down at the station,"

Elizabeth remembered the man who'd driven off with the car. But he couldn't have been her attacker. Neither could Guy, as he was still out working the crowd. "But I saw that deal happen. When I was with Jo and the boys. I thought it was weird that Guy just handed him the keys. Seemed a pretty trusting way to do business."

"I was standing right there when they arrested him. It was great. He tried to argue that the paperwork was in process, but nobody bought that. Ryland straight ignored him and read him his rights."

"Sounds like they're fairly confident."

"Even if you hadn't popped out of the trunk—"

"Rumble seat."

"Whatever. Anyway, when they searched the car and found the envelope, they had cause to search other cars. Envelopes in most of them. Half full of money, the other half full of drugs."

Kade glowered. "I knew Guy was up to something."

Elizabeth rubbed the fabric of the bedsheets together between her fingertips, thinking. "But my attacker wasn't Guy. He was blocks away."

Casey shrugged. "They've got Alma's video, likely someone casing the show from behind the scenes. Looking for an easy steal. The older beauties don't come with alarm systems. You've got to keep them locked up in a garage someplace."

Elizabeth bit the inside of her cheek and frowned. She'd been on her way to relay her own suspicions about Guy and his new business venture. He'd been at the stage with the crowd, though. Not in the holding lot. The far end of the show was for those who needed services like Kade's. Buyers and the sellers who were there to do the less glamorous side of business.

Business. Ponytail.

"Kade, you wouldn't happen to know a notary, would you? You know, someone who could verify sales."

Her boyfriend—she was starting to get used to that term—nodded. "'Course. At the garage, we've even got one in-house."

64

Wolf smoothed his mustache with the first two fingers of his hand. The whirr of the cassette recorder and the buzz of the fluorescent lighting served as white noise in the otherwise silent room.

"How did you know we'd found traces of peanuts on the mouthpiece?"

Elizabeth sat across from Wolf in a plush office chair. Deputy Ryland, notepad in his lap, sat next to her. He'd launched the digital recording on a laptop that rested atop the desk. Elizabeth's task was to recount the facts as she knew them, including those of her capture. The officers took notes while she spoke.

"Kade said Thor had all the symptoms of a severe allergic reaction when he collapsed on the stage. At Kade's party, he avoided all the foods with nuts, even the ones with that word in the name. My guess? When he put the trombone to his lips, it was over."

"But how did Becky know that?"

Elizabeth gave a little shrug. "She'd gone through all the files with a fine-tooth comb. Kade had asked her to, in a way. Managed the office while Raj was out. My guess is his employee information lists a peanut allergy."

Wolf scribbled a note on his desk pad. "You're right about her personal accounts, too. Up to her ears in debt. Claimed she took the job offer from Kade so she wouldn't have to sell the horses. This is all public information, by the way. Her house is in foreclosure."

"Drug running to play catch up," Ryland said. "It's not the first time we've seen it. But this is a new level."

Becky. Elizabeth underestimated the woman's need to keep her claws locked into Kade to maintain a hold on his business. It wasn't the day job or even lust. It streamlined access for moving drugs and cash. Raj had been collateral damage.

"Thor may have found out and wanted a cut. Or when Raj found the envelope, Becky panicked that there would be an investigation. She hired Thor to threaten Raj, then thought he'd give her up. My guess is that he'll be on the books as the mechanic for most of the cars—until Guy demanded Raj take over." Elizabeth ran her tongue over her teeth and considered the complications. "When Raj gave Guy an envelope full of cash, he probably freaked. He must have wanted to put the situation under his control."

"Becky claims she didn't want to hurt you. That she was only trying to keep you quiet until she could sweep the cars. Said she was going to ditch you in the park or someplace."

Elizabeth recalled the harsh warning she'd received while blindfolded. "I was a threat to her livelihood, and she did hurt me. But not permanently."

As the words left her mouth, Elizabeth realized they weren't true. She'd been shaken, terrified. Was so, still. It would take time to put distance between herself and the fear someone would again grab her off the street. She thought of Becky's own history. The son she'd lost. The woman had no love for Elizabeth, but did she spare her as a mother?

"Her life was falling apart at the seams. To her, you were the enemy, in a way," Ryland said.

"Straight out of the Cask of Amontillado. Only you escaped," Sheriff Wolf said after he pressed the button marked Stop. "'A wrong is unredressed when retribution overtakes its redresser. It is equally unredressed when the avenger fails to make himself felt as such to him who has done the wrong.'"

"I always liked Poe," Elizabeth said. "A mopey guy. But he was upfront with his feelings."

"Maybe I should become a teacher," Wolf said. "Jo would have my head, though. She's counting down the days until she gets to see me on a regular basis."

"There are worse things than having a spouse who wants you around," Elizabeth noted.

She thought of Kade. The soft kiss he'd brushed against her lips.

"Speaking of which," Wolf said. "I'm headed home. Can I give my honorary detective a ride?"

There was a knock at the door. "I think mine is here, but thanks."

"Come in," Wolf called.

Kade entered the room. Elizabeth reached for his hand.

"Ah, Mr. Michaels. I'll need your statement as well. Seems you're out one accountant."

"Slapped handcuffs on her myself," Ryland said. "You should have seen the look on her face. Like a firecracker, right before it explodes."

Clint shot Ryland a look of warning. "Deputy."

"What?" Ryland asked. "I'm simply stating facts."

65

Flames licked the split logs, crackling. Sparks zipped into the air and dissipated against the darkened sky. Kade draped a blanket around her shoulders before taking his own chair.

"They'll be here soon," Elizabeth said, glancing at her phone. "Casey said they're at the turn off."

Kade had built a fire pit in the space where they'd found Raj. He told her that if he didn't turn it into something good, the memory would haunt him.

He'd built the pit from a ring of cinder blocks, the first layer sunk halfway into the ground. He'd repurposed wine barrels into reclined seating. The chairs circled the snug fire, a gathering place.

Leia and Brutus, Chinook and husky, snoozed near the edge of the pit, bellies turned toward the heat. The former sled dog teammates were at home with each other, a reunion. "Like peanut butter and jelly," Kade said.

Benny and Rhett played at the edge of the firelight. Benny jabbered at his younger friend in a constant stream of discourse. The little boy relayed details about every leaf, moth, and stone in sight. Rhett, quiet, watched the older boy in unadulterated adoration. Elizabeth cherished their friendship.

"I've been thinking about what you said," Elizabeth said. "I'm going to try therapy for Rhett. If nothing else, it gives him an opportunity to interact with someone new. Maybe they'll help us learn something."

Kade looked over at Elizabeth. "I'll do a better job of keeping my opinions to myself. You don't have to defend your decisions as a mom to me. You're amazing, and you're doing an incredible job."

"Thanks," she said. "That's nice to hear."

"Glad I'm good for something," he teased. He held out his bottle, and she clinked hers against it.

"Relationships can't be one way. Or at least, not if they're going to last," Elizabeth said.

Kade paused, the rim of the bottle at his lips. "That's not something I learned as a kid. Wish I had." He took a drink, thoughtful.

"Don't worry," Elizabeth said. "I'm hardly the poster child for having all this figured out."

"I believe that if you're a decent person, good things will happen for you most of the time. Otherwise, what's this all for?" Kade took another swig.

"I struggle with that. Guy may have weaseled out of this, but he can't be innocent. People like him let other people get dirty while they maintain appearances."

"Oh, he's far from innocent," Kade said. He frowned, as though deciding what to say next. With a shake of his head, he leaned forward. "Open and honest, yes?"

Elizabeth nodded. Worry wrinkled her brow. "I'm listening."

"Guy is my father."

Elizabeth spit out her beer. She spluttered, then attempted to form a coherent sentence. "But you...but he...*what?*"

Kade looked down at his lap, then met Elizabeth's incredulous stare. "He and my mom...well. It was a while ago. She got pregnant, and he skipped out. Fast forward a couple decades and he ran into her in town. Only now he's some programmer, living in California. It's too late for her to get child support, and I'm a grown man who doesn't need or want a Daddy. So—I told him to stay away from me. He half listened. That was over fifteen years ago."

"But...the cars. His cars. Your shop? The envelope. Did the police know all this? You didn't *tell* me."

"It's not something I tend to open with. And yes, the police knew. I told them."

"But he's your *customer*. I don't understand." Elizabeth shook her head several times, as though willing the pieces to fall into place.

"When I wouldn't have anything to do with him, he took off for a couple of years. Then he was back. Mom said he'd bought a vacation place out here. Missed home or some nonsense like that. Started buying up cars, bringing them to the shop. He thought he could win me over through business. Truth is, I hated every moment, but I needed the work. One night after closing up, Raj and I had a couple beers. He told me his past and I told him mine. He took over managing Guy's account so I didn't have to."

"So, when he got attacked—you thought it was your fault?"

Kade nodded. "Ate me up. Still does, even though we know who did it. If I hadn't pushed Guy away, he wouldn't have brought shades of his dirty business to my shop. Raj wouldn't have bypassed me to return the envelope."

"I...don't know what to say." Elizabeth ran over the details of the last couple of weeks in her mind. Each hiccup was filled with new details, generating more questions.

"Can I ask a favor?"

At the sound of an approaching truck engine, the sleeping dogs each opened an eye. When a truck door slammed, Brutus got up, followed by Leia. They moved off down the driveway in a measured trot, side by side.

"I guess," Elizabeth said. Her feelings were a jumble on the inside. She attempted to process the information, make whole the gaps.

"I've been deep in this guilt for a couple of weeks. Can we take a break from Kade's Dark Past for a few more hours? I'd like to be a regular guy who invites his girlfriend and her family over for dinner, if I can. For tonight. When the boys go to bed, you can ask me anything you want, and I'll answer. Promise."

They'd planned to let Rhett stay the night on Benny's bottom bunk. Kade had shown Elizabeth the guest room where she'd dropped off her own small duffle on the spare bed. She'd hoped for a little alone time for herself and Kade after the boys went to bed, preferably under the stars. This discussion could change that...if she let it. "Actually, if it's alright with you, I'm okay letting the past be the past. For tonight."

Casey made his way to the fire pit, his arms full. His logger boots kicked up dust in his wake. "Hey, all. Grill ready? I'm starved."

"Yup." Kade gave Elizabeth's hand a grateful squeeze with his own, then held it up to tick items off on each finger. "I've got hot dogs, hamburgers, portobellos, and corn ready to go."

"We've got the watermelon," Casey said, setting a wrapped bowl on an empty chair. He bent over Elizabeth's chair to give her a hug. "How are you?"

"And the beer." Danny approached, a growler under one arm. He shook hands with Kade and took the seat next to Elizabeth. "Heard you got a little banged up. Brought you a consolation hazy for us to try. My latest experiment."

"Lucky me," she said. "What's in it?"

"Juniper. Kind of gin forward. Mushrooms, too."

"A woodland variety, then?"

"A celebration is in order. The car show is over, and I can have a life again," Kade said. He stood up. "I'll get the good glasses."

Casey quipped, "Digging out the mason jars?"

Elizabeth laughed, her cheeks turning pink. "Mason jars? I may be underdressed."

"You look perfect," Kade said, and bent down to kiss her. "Always do."

"Gross," Casey said. "Not in front of her big brother." Casey shook his head in mock disgust. "I'm going to find the boys." He reached out a hand to pull Danny up from the chair. They headed toward the barn and the sounds of play.

Alone again, the air between Elizabeth and Kade hung thick with anticipation. "I don't know what the future holds," he said, his voice barely above a whisper. "But I want it to be just like this."

"It holds us, together," Elizabeth said, a simple acknowledgement, and smiled. A breeze swept up around them. Her words carried across the prairie, up the towering mountains, and joined the wash of stars across the darkening sky.

***

Read the Series!

Subscribe to Erin's newsletter, get a free copy of *The Sheriff's Wife,* and more at erinlark.com

The Sheridan County Mysteries

The Sheriff's Wife(Prequel)

The New Teacher(#1)

The Sled Dog(#2)

The Dead Swede(#3)

The Master Mechanic (#4)

The Banjo Player (#5) — *Fall 2023*

Reviews help readers find books they'll enjoy and authors find people who love their stories. Please consider leaving a review on your favorite bookshop's website or with Goodreads.

Afterword

Decades ago I purchased a box the size of a board game. In it was a handful of character pamphlets, a set of directions, and a cassette tape. My first How to Host a Murder party was called Grapes of Wrath and I haven't looked back since. Nowadays, you can download electronic versions of materials, text your friends pre-party to get the game going, and launch the event with fully produced videos. What hasn't changed? The costumes, opportunity for custom menus, and problem-solving intrigue. If you've been considering giving them a try, you'll be able to find one for just about any party theme!

As a STEM teacher, I've loved teaching students to fly drones and introducing them to potential family-wage careers that leverage these tools. Ranching and farming are only a couple of industries that use drones, FAA drone pilots are employed in everything from surveying to Hollywood movies. Interested? Please check out your local laws for requirements and restrictions, then as they say—the sky is the limit!

The Karz Rod Run is a Sheridan County tradition each summer. Hobbyists and professionals from around the county and beyond descend on Main Street to appreciate the automobile in all its configurations. You'll find everything from the first Fords so the latest models and dozens of other vehicles from car makers around the globe.

Some of my favorite afternoons are spent with my father and my uncle, perusing the cars on display as a vintage car-loving family.

The Ford Model 40 is just one of many cars that came with a rumble seat option. Rumble seats predate cars, however, originating from horse-drawn buggy rides. Bumpy roads combined with wooden and metal wheels didn't make for the smoothest experience. Rumble seats in automobiles were intended to provide extra seating in a pinch. They were sometimes removed to make more space—a benefit in the times of bootleggers. Modern restorationists sometimes choose to reconfigure the insides of vehicles to reimagine space or use customizations to substitute for shortages of original parts, but many keep the rumble seat as a nod to the past.

About Erin

From the desert southwest, Erin fell in love with Sheridan County on the banks of Piney Creek as a child. An award-winning science teacher, avid archer, and hack watercolorist, she lives for the outdoors. Erin and her family divide their time between Wyoming, Washington, and Arizona because life is too short to play favorites.

The Master Mechanic

Book Four in The Sheridan County Mysteries series

by Erin Lark Maples

Cover designed by MiblArt.

www.ingramcontent.com/pod-product-compliance
Lightning Source LLC
LaVergne TN
LVHW091127080826
845145LV00008B/2066

* 9 7 8 1 9 5 9 1 1 6 0 5 9 *